50 Science ACTIVITIES

for Your Kindergarten Classroom

Photographs: pp. 4, 39: Ken Karp; p. 9, 21: James Levin; p. 55: Ross Whitaker.
Illustrations: Rita Lascaro; Cover, pp. 6–7, p. 8: Ellen Sasaki.
Book Design: Diane Cuddy.

Copyright © 1997 by Scholastic Inc.
All rights reserved. Published by Scholastic Inc.
Printed in the U.S.A.
ISBN 0-590-06254-9

5 6 7 8 9 10   3 4 5 6 7 8 9/0

Contents

5 0   S c i e n c e   A c t i v i t i e s

Introduction

ScienceDiscoveries

Kindergartners' innate curiosity about investigating their world makes them natural scientists.

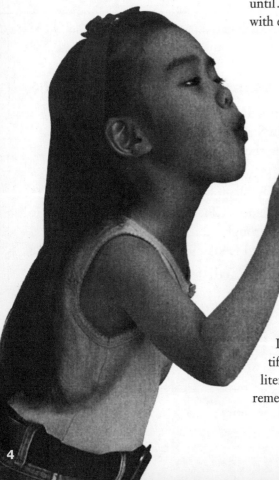

Kindergartners are born scientists, whose boundless curiosity and developing skills give them the motivation and capability to investigate and better understand their world.

Making Sense of the World

Do you remember learning about the four stages of the scientific method in junior high? Like adults, kindergartners observe, make predictions, experiment, and evaluate data every day. Just watch the process by which kindergarten children build a block tower. They add more and more blocks randomly until the tower inevitably falls over (observation). Filled with wonder, they think about how they could make the tower stay upright (prediction). They try different methods (experimentation) until…voilá…they discover that the blocks are more stable when they are flush with each other (evaluation).

Learning How to Think

To learn about science is to learn how to think. The abilities to comprehend, apply, analyze, synthesize, and evaluate are essential higher-order thinking and problem-solving skills that form the foundation of all learning. In kindergarten, when we teach science we are teaching the skills children will need throughout their lives to think about a problem and to explore its possible answers.

Building Bridges to Learning

Use the techniques presented in the science activities in this book to generate future science investigations. For example, you might adapt an activity about predicting which objects sunlight will shine through to one about predicting which materials will absorb water. Always be sure to involve your children so that your kindergartners will learn how to more formally apply the scientific method to whatever they do.

In kindergarten, you are never just teaching science! It is often difficult to identify an activity as a "science project" because it probably also incorporates math, literacy, and motor skills. As you help your children to "experience" science, remember that it's an approach to learning and life.

This book offers 50 developmentally appropriate science activities for kindergartners. The activities are grouped by theme and correlate to your children's growth throughout the year. They are also organized by season, making them easy to use to supplement your curriculum. As you adapt the activities for your children, remember that they are designed to be open-ended. First, provide the ideas and materials, then allow children to follow their interests and explore them freely. Integrate the activities with children's ongoing science explorations. You can make use of the science setup on the following pages as a guide for great materials and equipment to enrich your home base for science activities. Adapt the science journal ideas on page 8 for children's use in recording the results of their investigations. Refer to the index on pages 63-64 to find activities that encourage children to explore specific science skills and concepts.

Getting the most from the activity plans

The activity plan format is simple and easy to follow. Each plan includes most of the following:

AIM: The purpose of the activity; what children will do and learn.

MATERIALS: Basic materials and special items to gather. You will find that you have most of these on hand. The rest can be easily donated by parents or local businesses.

IN ADVANCE: Tips for materials to prepare or arrangements to make before introducing the activity.

WARM-UP: Ways to introduce the activity or underlying theme to the group. Open-ended questions help children think and talk about topics related to the activity.

ACTIVITY: Steps and suggestions for introducing materials, helping children get started, and guiding the activity in nondirective ways.

REMEMBER: Social/emotional, cultural, and developmental considerations; tips about ways to relate other skills and concepts to the activity theme; and occasional safety reminders.

OBSERVATIONS: Ideas and strategies for observing children that will help you understand their individual learning styles and guide, extend, or evaluate the activity.

SPIN-OFFS: Ideas for extending the activity into different curriculum and skills areas. Be creative: Add your own ideas and watch for those your children generate.

BOOKS: Children's books related to the activity or theme.

Colleagues, aides, student teachers, volunteers, and family members can all benefit from fun suggestions for child-centered science activities. So feel free to duplicate and share each plan for your program's use.

ScienceSetup

1 "Our Terrarium" chart shows children's observations of the earth-filled terrarium on the windowsill over a period of five days.

2 Related fiction and nonfiction books organized by topic help children with their research.

3 A question invites children to use creative and critical-thinking skills as they explore the nature of stones.

4 A display of children's handmade science books encourages the class to read each other's work and inspires children to create their own.

5 The large weather chart demonstrates a way to record both the weather and the passage of time.

6 Science-discovery trays provide a focused activity with a recording tool.

7 A magnifier suggests that children observe the classroom fish tank more closely. The book invites children to research more about the fish.

8 A box or basket keeps journals accessible to children.

9 Bulletin boards and the sides of storage shelves provide a good-size space to display children's predictions and explorations.

10 A small table provides space for children to draw and write in their science journals or lab books.

11 Materials that are well organized and attractively displayed encourage children not only to use them but also to take care of them.

12 Locating the sand/water table near or in the science area adds a new dimension to sand and water play.

ScienceJournals

Kindergartners' excitement about scientific discoveries is a natural motivator for recording their own investigations.

Children's ability to simultaneously understand concepts and represent information grows every day. At this stage, children's developing cognitive and literacy skills enable them to move beyond simply experiencing activities to recording their findings in science journals.

As you encourage children to keep journals, you invite them to reflect upon their new knowledge and skills. You'll also build a portfolio of each child's work that can become a valuable component of your assessment efforts.

The content of an activity will play a part in determining the best way to record information. As you make use of the activities in this book, encourage children to record their ideas in many ways. First try the journal tools illustrated below as whole-class or large group activities. This will give children new ideas to try out in their own journals.

Prediction Charts

Present some objects and ask a simple question, such as "What will light shine through?" or "Which objects will sink or float?" Invite children to state their predictions, and write them on the prediction side of the recording chart. As each item is tested, fill in the results side of the chart. Make the charts available in your science center for children to complete. Encourage them to add their own comments or experiment with chart-making in their science journals.

Measurement Graphs

Graphs enable children to chronicle events, from the growth of a bulb to the evaporation of a puddle. Children can use a nonstandard tool, such as a piece of string, to take each measurement, then attach it to the graph in sequential order to document change.

Pictorial Lists

Build language skills by encouraging children to list the items they measure or compare in pictorial and written form. They can then fill in their findings by using drawings, words, tally marks, or numerals. Children often enjoy keeping personal word lists in their own journals.

Field Books

Field-book pages invite children to draw and write about their observations of trees, animals, or weather. Such journals are appropriate for recording events in nature as well as the results of classroom experiments.

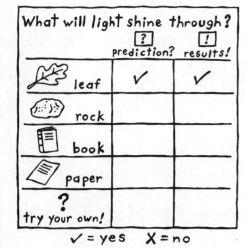

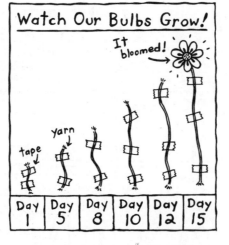

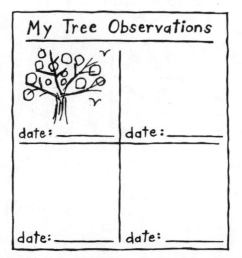

Activity Plans
for
Autumn

A t the beginning of the year, kindergartners are naturally drawn to explore the world from the perspective of their own bodies. By discovering all the things their bodies can do, they begin to see themselves as part of a living, ongoing science project. Whether they are learning about their bone structure or using their body as a unit of nonstandard measure, kindergartners are learning about their first tool of discovery…themselves.

Their experiences with changing autumn weather offer a perfect opportunity to help children move from self-understanding to using their senses to investigate their environment. Activities focused on observation, comparison, and prediction inspire kindergartners to learn more about the world they live in.

The new smells and tastes of autumn invite children to use their senses.

Throughout the Day

■ Encourage children to use their bodies as a unit of measure. How many feet long is the block area? How many giant steps to the cafeteria?

■ Introduce autumn words for describing the weather (crisp, brisk) and change (harvest, crimson).

Around the Room

■ Make mirrors available for children to use with both self-awareness activities and reflection experiments.

■ Create a seasonal corner of beauty for children to examine. Arrange autumn leaves, pictures, dried plants, abandoned nests, and other signs of the season in a place where children can enjoy their natural beauty.

"Me" Measuring

How big are you?

Materials

- construction paper
- markers or crayons
- scissors
- chart paper
- adding machine tape or ribbon

Aim

Children will make observations and predictions as they use their bodies as units of measure.

Warm-Up

Take off your shoe and trace your foot on a sheet of paper. Cut out the tracing and show children your "foot picture." Explain that you are going to use this to measure things in the room. Ask children to predict which items in the room are the same size as your foot. Let children each use the cut-out foot to test their hypotheses.

Activity

1 Have children each trace one hand and one foot on a sheet of construction paper and cut them out. Ask children to compare the hand and foot. Which one is longer? Wider? Are they bigger or smaller than the teacher's? Than their friends?

2 Invite children to make predictions about sizes and measurements. Ask, "What things in our room do you think are the same size as your foot? Which are smaller? Bigger?" Record each child's predictions on an experience chart.

3 Have children check out their guesses using their cut-out feet. Mark which predictions were correct on the chart. Then try the same procedure using the cut-out hands. Invite children to make other predictions. What objects are two or three hands long? Can they use manipulatives to build something that is two hands long? How many feet long is the trip from the classroom to the gym?

4 Use adding machine tape or ribbon to measure the children's height. Encourage children to take their "Me Strip" around the room to find things that are the same size, bigger, or smaller. Save the strips for comparison at the end of a year of growing.

Remember

- Be sensitive to children who may be uncomfortable about their size.

Observations

- What words do children use to compare sizes?

Books

Share these books about growth.
- *Peter's Chair* by Ezra Jack Keats (Harper & Row)
- *Where I Begin* by Sarah Abbott (Coward)
- *The Growing Story* by Ruth Krauss (Harper & Row)

SPIN-OFFS

- Have children take their "Me Strip" outside to find a "Me" tree, bush, weed, or plant that is the same size as their strip. Tie a piece of yarn and a name tag marked with their names around the plant. Throughout the year children can measure their feet and their trees periodically to see how fast they are growing in comparison to the tree. You can try this with indoor plants as well!

What's Inside of Me?

We all have bones.

Materials

- clean and boiled chicken, turkey, or fish bones
- sandbox
- pan balance

Aim

Children will use observation skills to learn about skeletons.

Warm-Up

Introduce children to the book *Look Inside Your Body* by Denise Patrick (Putnam) or other age-appropriate books about skeletons. Encourage them to look at the pictures and ask questions. Keep the book in your book corner for children to look through whenever they'd like.

Activity

1 Start a discussion about skeletons and bones at circle time. Invite children to try to feel the bones under their skin, especially the easy-to-find bones in their fingers, elbows, noses, chins, knees, and ankles.

2 Ask open-ended questions like "What has bones? Do trees? Do fish? Why do you think we have bones? What do you think would happen if we didn't have bones? What do you think bones look like? Do you think animals' skeletons look different from ours? Why or why not?" Allow plenty of time for discussion and sharing of ideas.

3 Introduce animal bones by hiding them in the sandbox. Invite children to go on an archeological "dig" in the box. Children can guess the kind of animal the bones came from.

4 Use the pan balance to compare the weights of different animal bones.

Remember

- At this time of year children may see pictures of skeletons hanging as decorations. Help them deal with scared or confused feelings by showing them what skeletons really are and explaining that everyone has one.
- Be prepared for some children to feel squeamish about touching bones. Don't force children to participate. Invite them to discuss their feelings about bones.

Observations

- Are children's comparisons and predictions guesses or fact-based?

Books

These books will enhance the experience.
- *Sandbox Scientist* by Michael Ross (Chicago Review Press)
- *My First Body Book* by Christopher and Melanie Rice (Dorling Kindersley Inc.)
- *Noses and Toes* by Richard Hefter (The Putnam Publishing Group)

SPIN-OFFS

- Place a model of a human skeleton or a medical diagram of a skeleton in your science area and observe children as they inquire about it. Encourage them to draw pictures of their skeletons or of dinosaurs' skeletons. Bring in a flashlight. Invite children to hold it very close to their hands and turn it on. They may be able to see the bones in their hands right through their skin! Explain what an X ray is and ask if children have ever seen one or had one.

Body Graphing

We can use our bodies to make a graph.

Materials

- masking tape
- large sheets of newsprint or white paper
- small squares of paper
- markers
- recorded music
- CD or cassette player

Aim

Children will use observation and comparison skills to find similarities and differences in each other.

In Advance

Prepare an open area. Starting from a blank wall, place strips of tape approximately 4 feet long on the floor. Create a picture for each attribute that will be graphed (boy/girl, hair color, eye color, sneakers/shoes/boots), and post them above the lines.

Warm-Up

Explain that a graph tells us the number of things in a group, and that they will use their bodies to make graphs.

Activity

1 Explain that together you will make a boy/girl graph using your bodies. Have children sit in the set-up dance area. Show them the tape lines on the floor and the signs on the wall. Ask some children to help you demonstrate how to stand on the line that describes them.

2 Play music and encourage children to move any way they wish. After a few minutes, tell children to freeze and then find the right (boy/girl) graph line and stand on it.

3 Have children reach across and hold hands with someone in the other line. Ask children who don't have a partner to raise their hands. "If there is nobody to hold hands with, what can you say about your line?"

4 Continue the routine, changing the pictures above the tape lines to represent new categories as children dance.

Remember

- Avoid categories that might make some children uncomfortable, such as height or weight.

Observations

- Do children suggest new categories or items to graph?

Books

Here are some books about differences.
- *We Are All Alike...We Are All Different* (Scholastic Inc.)
- *We Are All Different & That's Okay!* by Sheila Holden (Sheila Holden Books)
- *What Is Beautiful?* by Maryjean Watson Avery and David M. Avery (Tricycle Press)

SPIN-OFFS

- Use this technique with other science topics. Try graphing the characteristics of different stuffed animals or books. You might include rocks, blocks, or sunny-versus-rainy days. Explore math concepts by graphing the colors and patterns in children's clothes. Who's wearing stripes today? How about polka dots?

Trees Changing

Let's be tree experts.

Materials

- clipboards
- pencils
- chart paper
- paints
- construction or lined paper
- camera and film (optional)
- markers
- stapler

Aim

Children will make a class Big Book that records their observations of how trees change over time.

In Advance

Take children on a nature walk or ask them to look outside your window. Choose a nearby tree to observe. Name and discuss the different parts of the tree, such as branches, bark, leaves, and twigs. (If you go on a walk, let children collect leaves and twigs that have fallen to the ground to bring back with them.)

Activity

1 Over several weeks, take children on nature walks or set up a daily observatory by your window. Offer children clipboards and paper to write or draw about the changes they observe in the tree. Encourage children to photograph the tree is possible.

2 At the end of the fall, have children collect their drawings and observations to create a class book. Encourage children to refer to their recorded data, and invite them to share and discuss their tree observations. Ask children to dictate what they observed over time.

3 Discuss the sequence of the events and why sequence is important when writing a story: Write each observation on a separate sheet of chart paper, and place the sheets in sequential order.

4 Read each page aloud and invite children to add drawings and invented spellings. Include photos of the tree, if possible, and attach the pages to create a book. Include blank sheets for children to add further observations.

Remember:

- You can ask children to observe and record any type of seasonal change, no matter how small.

Observations:

- How do children record their observations? Do some need a lot of time to analyze the tree and process the information?

Books

Try these books about trees to enhance the experience.
- *Have You Seen Trees?* by Joanne Oppenheim (Scholastic Inc.)
- *When Autumn Comes* by Robert Maas (Henry Holt & Company)
- *Red Leaf, Yellow Leaf* by Lois Ehlert (Scholastic Inc.)

SPIN-OFFS

- Invite children to use found branches and leaves to create a large tree mural or sculpture. Encourage them to label the parts.
- Encourage children to collect colorful leaves and to save them by pressing them between sheets of wax paper. Display the leaves on the wall, or in the window, adding children's dictated comments.

Exploring Leaves

Leaves are "sense-sational"!

Materials

- heavyweight aluminum foil
- leaves
- newspaper
- construction paper
- finger paint
- white or colored paper
- paste

Aim

Children will use observation and comparison skills as they explore textures of leaves.

In Advance

Take a walk together outside to gather fall leaves. While children are leaf hunting, ask them to find leaves of different sizes and colors and compare them. How are leaves from different kinds of trees alike? How are they different?

Warm-Up

Gather children together to talk about the leaves they collected. Pass around a few leaves for children to touch. Together, compare the sizes, shapes, and textures of the different leaves. Encourage children to sort the leaves into piles of big and little leaves and to find other categories to sort them into.

Activity

1 Invite children to find the bumpy side of the leaf — the side with the raised veins. Demonstrate how to use fingers to spread paint on the leaf. Encourage children to compare the textures of the leaves and to predict which will make the best print.

2 Now invite children to predict which leaves will make an impression on the foil. Have children place each leaf on plain paper, paint-side down.

3 Invite children to place newspaper over the leaf and press on it to make a print.

4 Finally, ask children to place a piece of aluminum foil over a bumpy leaf and then gently press and rub to get a print. Which leaves left the best prints?

Remember

- Encourage children to describe how the leaves feel. Reinforce understanding by asking children to locate objects in the room that are bumpy, smooth, rough, or fuzzy.

Observations

- What comparative words do children use to describe the leaves?

Books

Share these favorite fall books.
- *All Falling Down* by Gene Zion (HarperCollins)
- *Frederick* by Leo Lionni (Pantheon)
- *The Wonderful Tree* by Adelaide Hall (Golden Press)

SPIN-OFFS

- Have each child roll out a piece of clay to a size a little larger than a leaf, and place a leaf on the clay bumpy-side down. Lay a sheet of waxed paper over the leaf and clay, and skim the rolling pin over the waxed paper so that the leaf sinks into the clay. Ask children to carefully remove the paper, pull off the leaf by the stem, and make a hole in the clay when it's still wet. Place the clay print in a sunny window. Insert a length of yarn when it's completely dry and hang it.

Planting Bulbs

Planting spring bulbs gives us something to look forward to!

Materials

- outdoor bulbs, such as tulip, daffodil, or crocus
- experience-chart paper, marker
- indoor bulbs such as paper-white narcissus or amaryllis
- small shovels, trowels, or big spoons
- flowerpots or bowls for indoor planting
- soil
- marbles or pebbles (optional)
- yarn
- watering can
- old plant catalogs
- tape

Aim

Children will see the difference between bulbs and seeds, and use comparison, measurement, and prediction skills.

Warm-Up

Gather children and examine a variety of bulbs. Discuss similarities and differences in size, shape, texture, and use. Record these similarities and differences.

Activity

1 Ask children to count the number of bulbs to be planted. Ask them to predict how many will sprout and bloom next spring. Record the predictions on the chart to refer to in the spring.

2 Invite children to choose a planting area outside the school that is safe from disruption, such as the edge of a fence or under trees. If you do not have an area outside, use only the indoor bulbs.

3 With children, read and follow the planting instructions on the package. Most bulbs need to be planted about 5 inches deep and about 3 to 5 inches apart. Replace the earth, press, and water well. If you're using different kinds of bulbs, label them.

4 Once the bulb sprouts, encourage children to use yarn to measure its growth weekly until it blooms. Attach the yarn lengths on paper in a left-to-right sequence to form a growth chart. Ask children to use another piece of yarn to predict how tall the plants will get. Compare their predictions with the actual outcome.

Observations

- Note children's measuring techniques. Do they understand how to use the yarn to measure from top to bottom? Do they seem to understand the concept of graphing?

Books

Try these books for more fun planting projects!
- *Growing Up Green* by Alice Skelsey (Workman Pub.)
- *All About Plants Activity Book* by Justine Korman (Scholastic Inc.)
- *Science Fun* by Imagene Forte (Incentive Pub.)

SPIN-OFFS

- Plant paper-white narcissus bulbs in soil in a flowerpot or in a shallow bowl of water (about 2 inches deep) filled with marbles or pebbles. Encourage children to observe and record the roots' growth.
- Provide children with art materials such as crayons, paper, paint, and clay, and encourage them to depict what the bulbs will look like when they grow next spring.

Set Up a Weather Station

Autumn brings big changes in weather.

Materials

- large blank calendar
- graph paper with large squares
- pictures of weather symbols, such as the sun, a cloud, an umbrella, and a snowflake
- construction paper
- crayons or markers
- tape

Aim

Children will use observation, prediction, problem solving, and recording skills.

In Advance

Create weather symbols and make a graph to record the month's weather.

Warm-Up

Look outside together and describe the weather today. Encourage children to describe different aspects of the weather. Is the day cloudy? Windy? Cold? Sticky? How might the weather change later in the day?

Activity

1 Introduce the weather calendar. Explain that each day children will observe the weather and help record it by placing a weather symbol in the matching box on the calendar. Place the appropriate symbol for the day's weather on the calendar together. Next, show children the graph. Explain that together you're going to record the number of sunny, cloudy, rainy, and snowy days you have all month. Each time someone puts a weather symbol on the calendar, they should add the same kind of symbol to the appropriate column on the graph.

2 As the days go by, help children compare the information they've gathered on the graph and the calendar. Encourage children to compare which kind of weather you've had the most of and the least of.

3 At the end of the month, save the graph so that children can compare it to graphs of future months. Throughout the year, collect the monthly graphs on a flip chart or in a class big book and store it in your science center. Refer to the previous months to analyze predictions.

Observations

- Do children take time to study the weather outside, or do they make quick judgments? What words do they use to describe the weather?

Books

Add these books to your weather station.
- *Evening Gray, Morning Red* by Barbara Wolff (Macmillan)
- *I Like Weather* by Claire Martin (Children's Press)
- *Flash, Crash, Rumble and Roll* and *Snow Is Falling* by Franklyn M. Branley (Thomas Y. Crowell)

SPIN-OFFS

- Talk about the appropriate clothing for various weather conditions. Fives may think that if it is sunny they can wear shorts — even if it's 50 degrees outside! Display a "weather doll" made of felt for children to dress each day.
- Invite a special classroom guest, like an astronomer, meteorologist, or family member who's a weather buff, to visit and answer children's questions about what causes the weather.

Appetizing Apples

So many foods are made from apples!

Materials

- several large sheets of graph paper
- variety of apple products, such as applesauce, apple juice, apple butter, and dried apples
- bread cut into bite-sized pieces
- plastic knives and spoons, paper plates and cups, napkins
- 3 apples —1 red, 1 yellow, and 1 green
- glue   ■ markers

Aim

Children will use comparison and evaluation skills as they explore different tastes.

In Advance

Prepare a taste-test graph to record children's likes and dislikes. Make two columns for each apple product, and paste a smiling face above one column and a frowning face above the other.

Warm-Up

Gather your group and show them the three apples. Talk about how they are alike and how they are different. Together, think of as many apple products as you can and discuss the ones children most like to eat.

Activity

1 Invite a few children to help you arrange an "Apple Buffet." Look at all the apple products. Encourage comparative and descriptive language as you notice the similarities and differences. Are apple pieces visible in any of the foods? How have the apples changed?

2 Help children match each product to the picture on the graph. Explain that they will use the graph to record which products they like and don't like.

3 Offer children a small amount of each food to taste, beginning with a piece of fresh apple. (Spread the apple butter on the bread pieces.) Discuss the tastes. Encourage children to use descriptive words like *sweet* and *sour*, rather than just *bad* and *good*.

4 Show children how to vote by placing a smiling-face circle in the columns of the foods they like and a frowning face in the columns of foods they don't like. Look at the graph together. Which foods do children like the most? The least?

Observations

- Do children have difficulty trying new tastes? What criterion do they base their comparisons on?

Books

These books will encourage more apple talk!
- *The Amazing Apple Book* by Paulette Bourgeois (Addison Wesley)
- *The Apple & Other Fruits* by Millicent E. Selsam (William Morrow & Co.)
- *Apple Tree* by Barrie Watts (Silver Burdett Press)

SPIN-OFFS

- Choose other foods, like breads, cheese, other fruits, corn, and rice, for children to taste, compare, and graph.
- Take a trip to a farm and go apple-picking. If possible, interview the farmer who grew the apples to learn more about how apples grow, what different kinds there are, and what you can make with them. Celebrate your trip with a tasty glass of cider!

Pumpkin, Pumpkin

Let's bake seeds and make shakes!

Materials

- cooking utensils: small saucepan, mixing bowl, cookie sheet, and blender
- paper cups and napkins
- sharp knife for adult use
- experience-chart paper
- marker
- measuring cups and spoons
- paper towels

Ingredients

- 1 fresh pumpkin
- 4 tbsp canned pumpkin
- 2 cups milk
- 2 bananas
- 1/4 tsp cinnamon
- 1–2 tbsp margarine
- graham crackers

Aim

Children will compare raw and cooked pumpkin.

In Advance

Make a picture recipe chart for the pumpkin milk shake recipe below.

Warm-Up

Gather children and invite them to watch as you cut off the top of a fresh pumpkin. Pass around the opened pumpkin and encourage children to use all their senses to observe the pumpkin, then invite them to describe it. Record their responses on experience-chart paper. Do the same with the canned pumpkin.

Activity

1 Tell children that they are going to make pumpkin milk shakes using the picture recipe chart.

2 Preheat the oven to 300°. Melt the margarine in a small saucepan. Together, pull the insides from your fresh pumpkin and separate seeds from string. Rinse the seeds in warm water and mix them in a bowl with the melted margarine. Spread the mixture on a cookie sheet and bake about 20 minutes until brown.

3 As the seeds bake, measure the milk, canned pumpkin, and cinnamon into a blender. Peel and slice the bananas. Add them to the mixture and blend until foamy.

4 Pour the shakes into paper cups. Serve them with roasted pumpkin seeds and graham crackers.

Observations

- What information do children use to make comparisons and draw conclusions?

Books

Read these vegetable books together.
- *Pumpkin Blanket* by Deborah Tumey Zagwyn (Celestial Arts)
- *The Rosy Fat Magenta Radish* by Janet Wolf (Little, Brown)
- *Pumpkin, Pumpkin* by Jeanne Titherington (Scholastic Inc.)

SPIN-OFFS

- Show children two different-sized pumpkins, and ask them to predict which will have more seeds in it. Surprisingly, the smaller one usually does!
- Have children save some raw seeds to compare to the cooked seeds. Ask them to predict how the raw seeds will change. Invite children to gather seeds from other kinds of vegetables and compare them to the pumpkin seeds.

Popcorn Predictions
How far will the kernel pop?

Materials

- popcorn popper (oil or hot-air)
- raw popcorn
- mural paper
- crayons

Aim

Children will use observation and prediction skills while preparing popcorn.

Warm-Up

Brainstorm a list of all the facts children know about popcorn. How does popcorn change when it's cooked? Where does it come from? Pass around both popped and unpopped kernels to aid in the discussion.

Activity

1 Explain that a prediction is a kind of guess. Tell children that they will be making a prediction about how far popcorn will pop out of the pan.

2 Place a large sheet of clean mural paper on the floor. Put the popcorn popper in the center of the paper, gather the children in a circle around the outside of the paper, and explain that they are going to pop the popcorn without a lid on the popper. Ask children to guess how far the popcorn will jump out the popper.

3 Draw a circle on the paper where you think most of the popcorn will land. Then, ask each child to draw a small circle to represent his or her prediction. Help children write their names or initials by the circles they have drawn.

4 It's time to pop the popcorn! Remind children to stand back because the kernels will be very hot when they pop. Children will love the excitement of finding out how close their predictions are. After the popcorn has popped, collect it and make another batch (with the lid on!) for snacking.

Remember

- Be sure to talk about safety precautions with hot appliances and food.

Observations

- Do children make a wide variety of predictions? Why do they think the popcorn will land in a particular place?

Books

Place these popcorn books in your science center.
- *Popcorn* by Millicent Selsam (William Morrow & Co.)
- *Mr. Picklepaw's Popcorn* by Ruth Adams (Lothrop, Lee & Shepard)
- *The Popcorn Dragon* by Catherine Woolley (Morrow Junior Books)

SPIN-OFFS

- Ask, "What would happen if it rained popcorn instead of rain?" Children can use plastic foam to make collage pictures of a popcorn-raining world!
- Have children play a popcorn movement game. After clearing a space, have them gather in the middle and pretend they are tiny unpopped kernels in a pan. As the pan heats up, they grow bigger and bigger until they start popping and jumping!

Candle Dipping
Let's see how candles are made!

Materials

- several pounds of paraffin or beeswax (available at many grocery stores)
- candles
- 2 large coffee cans
- stove or hot plate
- pot holders
- several milk cartons
- popsicle sticks
- candle wicking
- large pot
- large rubber basin

Aim

Children will watch a substance change from solid to liquid to solid. They'll also become aware of the importance of handling materials safely.

Warm-Up

Show children the candles you brought in, and ask them how they think candles are made. Break the candles in half so that everyone can see and touch the wicks inside. Show the paraffin or beeswax, and invite children to hypothesize about how they think these materials might be changed to create a candle shape.

Activity

1 Help children cut the wicking into 10" lengths and tie each piece to a popsicle stick. As you do this, talk about safety rules to observe around melted wax.

2 Away from children, melt the wax in a coffee can placed inside a pot of boiling water. Carry the can of wax carefully to a table, and place it in a rubber basin filled with about an inch of warm water.

3 Help each child hold a popsicle stick and carefully dip the wick into the wax for a second or two. Let children continue this process, taking turns, until their candles are about 1/2" thick.

4 Hang the candles to dry by laying the popsicle sticks across the top of an open milk carton.

Remember

- Be sure to use warm water in the basin; cold water will cause the wax to harden faster.
- You might need to reheat the wax between sessions.

Observations

- What properties of wax and what changes do children observe as they create candles?

Books

Enhance the experience with more craft activities.
- *The Little Hands Art Book* by Judy Press (Williamson Publishing)
- *Candles for Beginners to Make* by Alice Gilbreath (William Morrow & Co.)
- *Birthday Cake Candles* by Monica Weiss (Troll)

SPIN-OFFS

- Invite children to create free-form candles in the sandbox by making an indentation in wet sand, adding a wick, and pouring in hot wax.
- Provide modeling clay and suggest that children custom-make holders for their candles. Use the unlighted candles and holders in a special group activity or parade.

Activity Plans
for
Winter

As the year progresses, kindergartners become more and more interested in learning how things move and work. This is a good time to introduce experiences with the basic science concepts of temperature, time, sound, and volume. Open-ended experiments invite children to apply higher-order thinking and problem-solving skills to each new science concept they encounter. Through repeated experiences with physical science, children begin to apply scientific techniques and to analyze and synthesize information.

At this stage of the year kindergartners are ready to deal with more challenging concepts within the world of physical science. The focus of these activities is on observation, prediction, and experimentation with the process of change.

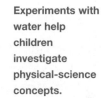

Experiments with water help children investigate physical-science concepts.

Throughout the Day

- Invite children to make predictions about daily events, such as what's for lunch or what they will see on a field trip.
- Discuss and observe change. Point out physical-science changes children can observe outside and inside the room. Introduce the concepts of freezing, melting, wet, and dry.

Around the Room

- Keep physical-science materials available for children to create their own extensions of science activities.
- Put out a number of different clocks and other timepieces for children to observe, use, and compare.

Experimenting With Time

How long does it take?

Materials

- variety of timers (windup kitchen timers, egg timers, sand timers, etc.)
- drawing paper
- paper cups
- fine sand
- markers
- pencils

Aim

Children will observe, predict, and record time.

Warm-Up

Talk about time. Ask, "How do people know what time it is? What would people do if there were no clocks?"

Activity

1 Help children compare the different timers. Talk about the different ways they work. Set two timers to go off in a minute and see if they both go off at the same time.

2 Help children make time predictions. For example, ask, "How many times can you jump up and down in 30 seconds?" Record children's predictions on a chart and then test them out together.

3 Explain that timers can also be used to figure out how long it takes to do something. Have children choose a timer to measure how long it takes to do various activities, like building a block tower, painting a picture, or singing a song.

4 Provide paper cups and pencils, and place sand in each cup. Help each child gently punch a hole in the bottom of his or her cup so the sand will slowly pour out. Ask, "What would happen if we put more holes in the cup? Will the sand timer empty faster or slower?" Help children add holes and then time the sand as it pours out. They might also compare sand timers with different numbers of holes.

Remember

- Focus on temporal terms throughout the week. Refer to the clock, use words like *yesterday* and *today*, and point out events that take a long or a short time.

Observations

- What words do children use to describe time? Do they understand the purpose of a timer?

Books

These books will inspire more thought about time.
- *All Kinds of Time* by Harry Behn (Harcourt Brace Jovanovich)
- *Do You Know What Time It Is?* by Roz Abisch (Prentice Hall)
- *It's About Time* by Miriam Schlein (Addison-Wesley)

SPIN-OFFS

- Make another sand timer by taping a paper cup with one hole in it inside a glass jar. Children can observe the timer and watch time pass as the sand piles up. Use a timer to help you place enough sand in the cup to make it last exactly one minute, two minutes, or three minutes. Try using this to time your next cleanup!
- Talk about the importance of time in cooking. You might boil pasta for 5 minutes and 20 minutes and compare the tastes.

An Observation Game

Observing is especially fun with this unusual game!

Materials

- adult (parent or aide) dressed in a very strange costume and carrying odd objects
- experience-chart paper
- markers

Aim

Children will practice observation and memory skills.

In Advance

Arrange for an adult to visit your program dressed in a very strange costume.

Warm-Up

Tell children that today at circle time they will meet a unique visitor. Explain that this person is just a little unusual in a fun way. Ask children to look at the visitor carefully and see how many strange things they notice about her. Present the visitor in a funny, light way so that children will not be frightened when she arrives.

Activity

1 Invite the visitor into the room and watch children's reactions. Invite children to ask the visitor questions about where she lives, what she likes to eat, and what her hobbies are. Let them observe the visitor for a minute or two and then say good-bye.

2 Encourage children to take time to really think about what they saw, and ask them to share what they noticed about the visitor. Make an experience chart of children's observations. Ask, "What made that person unusual?"

3 When children run out of observations, ask them to think about specifics, such as the colors, shapes, and patterns of the clothing the visitor was wearing or of the objects she was carrying. Add these to your chart.

4 Bring the visitor back in. First have children look for things they forgot or missed. Then ask them to check their observations against the real thing!

Remember

- Some children may be frightened by someone too strange-looking. Be sensitive to children's fears.

Observations

- What are the main characteristics children observed — large abnormalities or small?

Books

Here are some books about the importance of looking carefully.

- *What Is Your Favorite Thing to See?* by Myra Gibson (Grosset & Dunlap)
- *I Spy* by Jean Marzollo (Scholastic Inc.)
- *Take Another Look* by Tana Hoban (Greenwillow Books)

SPIN-OFFS

- Try observing and describing each other. Together, choose one child at a time and make a chart with a collection of the observations children make, such as "He has red hair. He is wearing blue jeans and a green shirt. He smiles a lot." Add unique and warm observations of your own to help each child feel special. Post the chart in your language area and entitle it "We Are All Special."

Magnet Mania
Opposites attract in this activity!

Materials

- variety of magnets
- masking tape
- 2 trays
- chart paper
- markers
- magnetic items such as paper clips, screws, brass fasteners
- nonmagnetic items such as buttons, feathers, sponges

Aim

Children will problem-solve and build observation and prediction skills as they experiment with magnets.

Warm-Up

Invite children to go on a magnetic scavenger hunt. Give each child a magnet and a few strips of masking tape. Ask children to explore the room to find objects that are and aren't magnetic. Tell them to put a piece of tape on items that are magnetic. Walk around the room together, and ask children to name the magnetic items they found. Make a list of these objects and talk about how they are the same or different.

Activity

1 Invite children to gather around a table. Show them each magnet and examine its size and shape. Ask children to think about which magnets are stronger than the others. Discuss their hypotheses.

2 Place the magnetic and nonmagnetic items and two trays in the center of the table. Label one tray "Yes" for items children think will be attracted to the magnets and the other tray "No" for items they think will not be attracted.

3 Invite children to use the magnets to test their predictions. As they experiment, ask them to place the magnetic objects in the "Yes" tray and the nonmagnetic objects in the "No" tray.

4 Ask children to pair up to play a magnetic guessing game. Children can work together to find more magnetic objects around the room.

Observations

- Do children find other ways to use magnets? How do they test their hypotheses?

Books

These books will provide more information about magnets.
- *Look at Magnets* by Rena Kirkpatrick (Raintree Publisher Inc.)
- *All About Magnets* by Stephen Krensky (Scholastic Inc.)
- *The Mystery of Magnets* by Melvin Berger (Newbridge Inc.)

SPIN-OFFS

- Invite children to make homemade magnets. Help each child straighten out a paper clip. Ask them to rub a magnet over their paper clip at least 25 times in the same direction. Then let them experiment with these "attractive" clips.
- Provide children with compasses and encourage them to find where north is. See if the compass needle changes direction if children place a magnet close to it.

Fill 'er Up

There's lots to learn just filling containers!

Materials

- sand table or dishpan of sand
- variety of containers, including different-shaped plastic bowls, bottles, measuring cups, cardboard boxes
- markers
- experience-chart paper

Aim

Children will explore the concept of volume.

Warm-Up

Talk about predictions. Explain that a prediction is like a guess that people have thought about. For example, the weatherperson makes a prediction about the weather based on things that he or she has observed before. Brainstorm some ways children make predictions at home and in different areas of the room.

Activity

1 Introduce the various containers and explain to children that they will experiment with filling them with sand. Encourage children to fill and dump as much as they like. Then gather children (and the containers) for another discussion. Which containers are big and which are small? Which are heavier and which are lighter?

2 Make a chart with a simple outline picture of each container. Invite children to predict which container will hold the most sand. Have each child make a mark on the chart next to the picture of the container he chooses.

3 Have children take turns filling the containers with measuring cups of sand. Encourage everyone to count together as each container is being filled. Compare the results with the predictions and mark the outcome on the chart. Have children repeat the procedure to predict (and test) which container will hold the smallest amount of sand.

4 Ask children to predict which of the containers will hold the same amounts and why.

Remember

- The object of this activity is to help children learn to observe and make thoughtful guesses.

Observations

- Do children understand the concept of filling containers to the top? Do they understand the meaning of full?

Books

Try these books about messy play!
- *Mudpies to Magnets* by Williams, Rockwell, and Sherwood (Gryphon House)
- *What Will Happen If...?* by Sprung, Froschl, and Campbell (Educational Equity Project)
- *Art & Industry of Sandcastles* by Jan Adkins (Walker & Company)

SPIN-OFFS

- Collect boxes of similar sizes but different shapes. Ask children to predict whether the boxes will hold the same amount of sand, more, or less. Have children experiment with the different boxes and test out their predictions.
- Provide materials that sand will sift through, such as colanders, funnels, screens, and strainers. Encourage children to test predictions about how quickly sand will flow through them.

How Much Is There?

Water and sand are perfect partners.

Materials

- jar filled with raisins
- different-sized plastic containers
- tub filled with water
- water
- measuring cups
- sand
- chart paper
- crayons or markers

Aim

Children will observe, predict, experiment with, and evaluate volume.

In Advance

Prepare a prediction chart by drawing pictures of the jar and containers at the top of a page of chart paper. Underneath each picture, make two columns, one for children's predictions and the other for results.

Warm-Up

Explain that a prediction is a guess based on the things you watch and see. Then ask children to predict how many raisins are in the jar. Record their predictions on the chart paper. Open the jar and count the number of raisins. Ask children to talk about whether their guesses were too high or too low.

Activity

1 Show children the collection of plastic containers. Ask them to pick out the ones they think need the most cups of water and fewest cups of water to be completely full.

2 Invite children to take turns predicting just how many cups of water will fill each container. Help children record their predictions in the appropriate column of the chart.

3 Test out the predictions by helping children make a mark on the paper each time they add another level cup of water to a container.

4 Compare the predicted amount with the actual amount measured. Ask, "How close was your guess? Was it too high or too low?" Encourage children to try different containers and to construct their own theories of volume.

Observations

- Note the science vocabulary children use.

Books

These books offer more science ideas!
- *The Kids' Science Book* by Robert Hirschfeld and Nancy White (Williamson)
- *Simple Science Experiments With Straws* by Eijo Orii and Masako Orii (Gareth Stevens)
- *Make It Change* by Dorling Kindersley (R. R. Bowker)

SPIN-OFFS

- Use masking tape to create three different-sized rectangles on the floor. Invite children to predict how many unit blocks (same size) will fill the squares. Which will need the most? Chart it. Then test the predictions.
- If there is snow outside, try comparing the number of cups of snow to the number of cups of water it would take to fill a container. Record your results.

Shake a Sound

Let's experiment with sounds!

Materials

- experience-chart paper
- variety of containers with lids, such as:
  oatmeal tubs, milk cartons, coffee cans
- items to make sounds, such as:
  gravel, buttons, bells
- markers

Aim

Children will develop listening skills as they create, compare, and classify sounds.

In Advance

Gather the "sound" materials and place in separate bowls.

Warm-Up

Ask children to sit very quietly and close their eyes. Together, listen for sounds in your room, the building, and outside. Discuss which sounds are loud and which are soft. Then encourage everyone to think of other loud and soft sounds. Record their ideas.

Activity

1 Show children the different sound materials you set out. Encourage them to guess which ones will make the loudest and softest sounds when shaken in a container.

2 Invite each child to choose one container and one type of item. Show everyone how to place their item in the container, close the lid, and shake it. Listen together and compare the sounds. Which are loud? Which are soft? Are some in between?

3 Suggest that children choose another container and item and repeat the process. They might like to choose their own sound materials from around the room.

4 Ask children to sort and classify their sound containers in different ways, such as loud and soft or scratchy and smooth. Encourage them to try different combinations.

Remember

- If you have a mixed-age group, supervise younger children very carefully. Make sure your sound materials pass the choke-tube test.

Observations

- Do some children have difficulty distinguishing between sounds?

Books

Here are some wonderful books about sounds.
- *Hearing* by Maria Rius, J. M. Parramon, and J. J. Puig (Barron)
- *Plink, Plink, Plink* by Byron Baylor (Houghton Mifflin)
- *Too Much Noise* by Ann McGovern (Scholastic Inc.)

SPIN-OFFS

- Send children home with a small paper bag. Ask them to find something at home that makes a sound and place it in the bag. At group time, ask each child to make the sound without showing the object they found while others guess what it is.
- Encourage children to use the shakers they created to experiment with rhythms and beats while listening to music.

Blocks and Boards

How do balls roll down ramps?

Materials

- 2 boards of equal length
- hollow cardboard blocks or unit blocks
- toy vehicles
- small rubber balls
- tape
- small toys or objects

Aim

Children will experiment with motion and inertia.

In Advance

Set up a ramp in the block area using a board. Place a hollow block or stack of unit blocks under one end of the board, lifting it about 12 inches off the floor. Park cars and trucks nearby.

Warm-Up

Show children the balls, cars, and trucks, and tell them that you'll return later. Observe how children use the materials. Do they roll the balls and cars down the ramp? Do the cars roll smoothly or fall off the side? Do children add walls to the side or blocks to the bottom of the ramp?

Activity

1 After a while ask, "What happened with the cars and balls? Will they stay on the ramp?" Suggest that children use the other board to make a second, higher ramp next to the first one.

2 Encourage each child to predict which ramp will make the cars run faster. Then set the cars on the ramps and let them go! Ask children to tell why they think the higher ramp was faster.

3 Now ask children to guess which height ramp will make the ball roll farther and to mark the spot on the floor with tape. Then encourage them to test their predictions.

4 Have children set up small toys at the end of the ramps to knock down. How high or low will the ramps have to be for the balls to reach the targets?

Remember

- Introduce different aspects of ramp play over a few days so that children can experiment with ideas.

Observations

- Do children become frustrated, or do they create solutions to their problems?

Books

These books will inspire more ramp-building.
- *New Road* by Gail Gibbons (Thomas Y. Crowell)
- *Changes, Changes* by Pat Hutchins (Macmillan)
- *If You Look Around You* by Fulvio Testa (Dial Books)

SPIN-OFFS

- Attach mural paper to boards and place them on newspaper. Dip wheels or balls in tempera, and roll them down the board to create a visual representation of motion!
- Ask children to find ramps outside — a slide, a sloped sidewalk, a stair rail — and use them to experiment with the speed of bigger objects, including themselves!

A January Garden

It's spring inside!

Materials

- seed catalogs
- construction paper and paste
- clear-plastic cups
- window boxes, fish tubs, or plastic-lined cardboard boxes
- potting or local soil
- small stones or gravel
- trowels or large spoons
- watering can

Aim

Children will use observation and experimentation skills as they plant an indoor garden and record its growth.

Warm-Up

Make a list of the hardiest flowers and vegetables in your area. Together with children, choose seeds from a catalog.

Activity

1 Cut out pictures of flowers and vegetables from catalogs, and paste them on construction paper to make a map of your planned garden. Read the planting instructions together.

2 Together, fill the bottom of the tubs or boxes with pebbles or gravel, then add the soil. Help children carefully plant seeds in the soil, and then water. To observe growth closely, try planting a few seeds on damp paper towels in the clear-plastic cups.

3 When seedlings reach about one inch in height, thin them according to directions on the package. Explain that it's important to thin plants so that there is room for growth.

4 Invite children to keep a weekly journal in which they draw the changes they observe. Provide pieces of yarn for children to measure plant heights weekly, and help children paste these in a row on a page of their journal.

Remember

- In their eagerness to care for plants, children often overwater them. Talk about how this can be harmful, and perhaps arrange an experiment to show the effects of too much water, using plants in small cups.

Observations

- Observe children's fine-motor skills as they handle small and delicate items.

Books

Here are a few good books about planting and growing.
- *The Plant Sitter* by Gene Zion (Scholastic Inc.)
- *Eric Plants a Garden* by Jean Hudlow (Albert Whitman)
- *Up Above and Down Below* by Irma E. Webber (William R. Scott)

SPIN-OFFS

- Create a watering experiment. Place thinned seedlings in cups, then water some too much and others not at all. What happens? Record your results.
- Make a seedling greenhouse. First, take a carton and help your children cut out windows on every side. Have children tape plastic wrap over the windows to create a warm, moist place for young plants.

Temperature Time
Let's feel the heat!

Materials

- water
- 3 large bowls
- metal spoons
- paper cups
- thermometers
- chart paper
- markers

Aim

Children will explore temperature changes.

Warm-Up

Talk about hot and cold. Ask children to demonstrate how they can make their hands feel warmer. You may suggest blowing warm air on them or rubbing them together. Next, have children make their hands cold by fanning them.

Activity

1 Talk about the temperature changes that take place where you live. Is it hot or cold outside now? How do we know when the weather is cold or hot?

2 Fill two paper cups with water, one quite warm, the other cold. Invite children to feel the outside of the cups and to choose the one they think is warmer. Mark a red dot on the cup they choose. Use the metal spoons as thermometers. Pass the three spoons around so that each child can feel whether they are hot, warm, or cool.

3 Ask a child to place one spoon in each cup and leave one out of the water. Have children predict whether the wet spoons will change temperature and, if so, how. Keep the spoons in the water for one minute. Then remove them and compare them with the dry spoon.

4 Fill three bowls with cold, room-temperature, and warm water. Have one child put a hand in the cold-water bowl and describe how it feels. Then, leaving that hand in the cold water, have him place his other hand in the warm-water bowl and describe how it feels. Finally, have the child put both hands in the bowl of room-temperature water. Ask, "How do your hands feel now?"

Remember

- Do not make water too hot for children to touch.

Observations

- What comparative and descriptive vocabulary do children use while experimenting?

Books

Here are some great books about temperature.
- *Hot & Cold* by Neil Ardley (Franklin Watts Inc.)
- *Why You Feel Hot, Why You Feel Cold: Your Body's Temperature* by James Barry (Little, Brown)
- *Science Fun* by Imogene Forte (Incentive Publications)

SPIN-OFFS

- Fill four paper cups with four kinds of water very warm, warm, cold, and cold water with ice cubes. Have children feel the outside of each cup and arrange them in order from hottest to coldest. Next, put a thermometer in each cup and wait a few minutes. Remove and compare the different levels of mercury. Record the temperatures.
- Ask children to recall times their parents or the doctor took their temperature. What did they learn?

It's Melting!
What happens to ice?

Materials

- chart paper
- ice cubes
- plastic containers
- aluminum foil
- plastic wrap
- marker
- water
- paper cups and plates
- piece of cloth

Aim

Children will investigate the fastest and slowest ways to melt an ice cube.

Warm-Up   *circle*

Gather children for a discussion about melting. Ask, "What happens when you put ice in a glass of water? What happens when you bring a snowball inside?" Give children plenty of time to share their ideas.

Activity

1 Ask children to think of different ways to melt ice cubes. Record their ideas on chart paper, and then ask them to predict which method will work the fastest and which the slowest. Try the methods for which you have materials. For example, place an ice cube in a container of cold water, one in hot water, and one in sand or snow.

2 Wrap the ice cubes in different materials, such as aluminum foil, plastic wrap, and cloth, then invite children to predict which cubes will melt the fastest.

Record predictions, experiment, and then invite children to refer to the predictions. Talk about which methods work the best and star those on the chart.

3 Place ice cubes around the room. Ask children to help you decide where to test the cubes, such as on a sunny window, in a refrigerator, and near a heater. Ask them to rank the places by how fast they think the ice will melt in each spot. Record the predictions.

4 When the cubes have all melted, check the chart. Discuss why a particular cube melted faster than another. Encourage all children to share their conclusions.

Remember

- Keep the focus on the conditions that are needed for objects to melt — mainly a heat source.

Observations

- Are children's predictions random guesses or are they based on experience?

Books

These books about water and ice will enhance the experience.
- *All Wet! All Wet!* by James Skofield (HarperCollins)
- *Ice Is... Whee!* by Carol Greene (Children's Press)
- *Water Is Wet!* by Sally Cartwright (Coward, McCann & Geoghegan)

SPIN-OFFS

- On a snowy day, empty the water table and fill it with snow. Ask, "How much water will a box full of snow make?" Have children mark the level of snow in the box with tape or a marker, and then mark their predictions in a different color. Compare the marks to the level of the melted water.

Oodles of Noodles

Bubble, boil — and watch things change!

Materials

- hot plate or stove-top burner
- various kinds of noodles
- spoons, forks, and napkins (one for each child)
- large glass pot
- pot holders
- water
- colander
- plastic cup
- small bowls

Aim

Children will observe changes in water and will use their senses to examine raw and cooked noodles.

In Advance

Set up the hot plate on a countertop away from children, but where they can easily see it. Place the bowls, noodles, and pot of water on a table.

Warm-Up

After children have washed their hands, invite them to gather around the table. Offer each child a few raw noodles and talk about them together. How do the noodles feel? How do they smell? What shapes are they? How do they taste?

Activity

1 Ask whether anyone has ever seen noodles being cooked. What do you need to cook noodles?

2 Put the glass pot on the hot plate or stovetop, and ask children to observe what's happening to the water from time to time. Remind them not to get too close.

3 When the water reaches a full boil, add the noodles. Turn the temperature down.

4 When the noodles are done, pour them into the colander. Pour cold water on them, and drain. Place in bowls and encourage children to touch and taste the noodles. How have they changed? Record children's responses.

Remember

- Make sure that children stay safely away from the heat but can still see inside the pot.

Observations

- Note children's comments about boiling water for prior knowledge you can use to extend discussions.

Books

Here are some more books about cooking!
- *Pasta Factory* by Hana Machotka (Houghton Mifflin Company)
- *Is There an Elephant in Your Kitchen?* by Ethel and Len Kessler (Simon & Schuster)
- *Pretend Soup* by Mollie Katzen and Ann Henderson (Tricycle Press)

SPIN-OFFS

- What else do we boil water for? Explore dying cotton fabric or yarn with natural dyes by boiling such things as onion skins, beet juice, or instant coffee!
- Experiment with boiling eggs for different lengths of time, from 1 minute to 10. What happens when you break an egg into boiling water? When the egg is cracked?

Ice, Water, and Salt

What makes ice melt fastest? Experiment and see!

Materials

- experience-chart paper and markers
- 3 aluminum pie plates
- 3 paper cups
- water
- table salt or rock salt
- optional: egg timers, thermometers, and magnifying glasses

Aim

Children will experiment with different ways to melt ice.

In Advance

Make a predictions chart. Across the top, write, "Which will melt ice fastest?" Make three columns and label them for the three methods children will use to melt ice: water, salt, and water mixed with salt. Then fill three aluminum pie plates with water and freeze them overnight.

Warm-Up

Talk about ice and melting. If you live in an area where there are winter storms, talk about the different methods people use to melt ice on sidewalks.

Activity

1 Together, fill one paper cup with cool water and another with table salt or rock salt. In a third cup, mix water and about 1 tablespoon of salt. Ask children to predict which of these materials will melt ice fastest. Then invite them to mark their predictions on the chart.

2 Bring out the three pie plates filled with ice. Use one plate to try each melting method and encourage children to observe the effects. What's happening?

3 Watch to see which makes a hole in the ice first, which second, and which third. Fill in the results on the chart and compare to children's predictions.

4 If the weather is cold enough in your area, pour some water on the ground in a safe spot. After the water has frozen, add salt and/or water and see if the ice melts faster outside or inside. Set out timers, thermometers, and magnifying glasses for children to use in their experiments.

Remember

- Discourage competition about who was right.

Observations

- How do children verbalize the changes they observe?

Books

Try these books about seasonal changes.
- *When Will It Snow?* by Syd Hoff (HarperCollins)
- *Seasons* by John Burningham (Bobbs-Merrill)
- *Ice Is...Whee!* by Carol Greene (Children's Press)

SPIN-OFFS

- Mix salt water and food coloring. Use eyedroppers to drop colored salt water onto a large block of ice. Watch rainbow-colored caverns melt through the block and mix colors!
- Freeze plain water and salt water in ice cube trays. Time which takes longer to harden and which takes longer to melt.

Lifting Water

Moving water can be an "uplifting" experience.

Materials

- water table or tubs
- water
- smocks
- different lengths and sizes of straws, tubes, and plastic cups
- basters, sponges, paper towels, and pumps
- siphon (long plastic hose)

Aim

Children will practice eye-hand control and prediction-making skills as they use their fingers to draw water into straws or tubes.

Warm-Up

Talk about moving water. How do you use a garden hose? What is used to put out fires? Invite children to suggest a variety of ways people can move water.

Activity

1 Fill your water table or tubs to a depth of 1 inch. Offer children straws, cups, and tubes, and suggest they use a straw and their fingers to get water into their cups. Talk about possible methods and encourage children to experiment to see if their suggestions work. If necessary, demonstrate that when they place their finger over one end of the straw, they can transport water through the tube.

2 Invite children to practice transporting water into the small containers. Encourage children to make predictions and to test them.

3 Over time, put out basters, sponges, paper towels, and pumps from empty liquid soap dispensers. Invite children to experiment with these materials.

4 Introduce the siphon. Explain that people use it to move water from one place to another — when cleaning a fish tank, for example. Demonstrate its use and invite children to experiment with it at the water table.

Remember

- Remind children not to put straws into their mouths to suck water or blow into the water table.

Observations

- This activity may be very difficult for some children. Watch for frustration levels and lend a hand if needed!

Books

These books have simple water experiments.
- *Experiments With Water* by Ray Broekel (Children's Press)
- *Simple Science Experiments With Straws* by Eijo Orii and Masako Orii (Gareth Stevens)
- *Simple Science Experiments With Water* by Eijo Orii and Masako Orii (Gareth Stevens)

SPIN-OFFS

- Use tempera paint thinned with water in cups to make "lifted paint" pictures. Children can use straws and their new skill to pick up paint and drop it on paper to create a recording of the process!
- Encourage children to look at home for materials that might lift water and to bring them to school to test.

Wood on the Water

Experiments with buoyancy.

Materials

- different types of wood in various sizes
- water table or basins filled with water
- glue
- nails
- hammers

Aim

Children will predict whether materials will sink or float.

Warm-Up

Add a few small wood scraps from your woodworking area to your water table as accessories. Encourage children to investigate what happens to the wood when it gets wet. Add some wood pieces to the scraps.

Activity

1 Gather again around the water table. Invite each child to choose one wood piece and to predict whether it will sink or float. Then put all the pieces in the water and see what happens.

2 Encourage children to think of ways to use the nails and glue to change the wood and to predict whether the changes will make the wood sink or float. To promote reasoning skills, encourage children to talk about the reasons for their predictions.

3 Now let them test their ideas. Invite two children at a time to use nails, glue, and woodworking tools to change the wood in any ways they choose. When they finish, encourage them to take the wood to the table to see if it sinks or floats.

4 Next, encourage children to explore concepts of weight and density by asking "what can you add to make your boat sink?" Encourage them to test their ideas by adding small objects they find around the room.

Remember

- Follow your regular safety rules for woodworking. Only two children should use the woodbench at one time, and they should always wear goggles when sanding, hammering, or sawing. Be sure all wood is sanded smooth.

Observations

- Listen carefully to the reasons children offer for their predictions. It will give you an interesting window into their thinking.

Books

Here are some fun books about boats.
- *Sheep on a Ship* by Nancy Shaw (Houghton Mifflin)
- *Mr. Gumpy's Outing* by John Burningham (Henry Holt)
- *Who Sank the Boat?* by Pamela Allen (Putnam Publishing Group)

SPIN-OFFS

- Will a piece of clay or plasticine float? Try dropping a glob of clay into the water table. Ask, "How can you change the clay to make it float?" Invite children to reshape clay into a floating shape.
- Invite a special guest who works with boats to visit and answer children's questions. Is it important not to bring too many things aboard? What makes the boat float?

Magnifier Magic

Can water make things look bigger?

Materials

- assortment of plastic magnifying glasses
- plastic wrap
- newspaper
- small objects such as pennies, feathers, marbles, and shells
- watering cans or small containers filled halfway with water

Aim

Children will experiment and predict as they learn about magnification.

Warm-Up

Bring a magnifying glass to group time. Have children brainstorm its identity and use. Then show children a small item like a penny, and ask, "What will happen to the penny when I look at it through the magnifying glass?" Pass around the magnifier and the penny so that each child can take a look.

Activity

1 Put out the magnifiers and a collection of small objects for children to explore. Ask them to try to predict what each of the items will look like when it's magnified. Have them look at the item with the magnifying glasses. Were their predictions close?

2 Invite children to observe their hair and skin through the magnifiers. Ask, "How does your hair/skin look different?" Next, ask children to observe other objects in the room. Have them bring objects back to share.

3 Lay out a piece of newspaper. Ask, "How will the letters look if we put a magnifying glass over them?" Test out their predictions. Then hold up a piece of plastic wrap, and invite children to observe the letters through the wrap. (The letters will be the same size.)

4 Ask, "What do you think will happen to the letters if we put some water on the plastic wrap?" Encourage children to experiment.

Remember

- Encourage children's interests as much as possible by supplying a variety of materials and time to experiment.

Observations

- How do children explain what they are seeing?

Books

These books will help introduce magnification.
- *Take Another Look* by E. Carim (Prentice-Hall)
- *What Is It?* A Book of Photographic Puzzlers by Joan Loss (Doubleday)
- *All About Magnifying Glasses* by Melvin Berger (Scholastic Inc.)

SPIN-OFFS

- Help children make their own magnifiers by filling sealable plastic bags with different amounts of water. Encourage them to note how much larger the letters lock through them.
- Invite a staff member who wears eyeglasses to talk about why he wears them and how the glasses help. Let children look carefully through the glasses.

Dip and Design
New ways to create with colors!

Materials

- oil-based paint (2 or 3 colors)
- shallow pan
- cooking oil
- white paper
- wire-screen strainer
- popsicle sticks
- water
- eyedropper
- large sticks of colored chalk
- small bowls

Aim

Children will use hypothesizing, experimenting, and synthesizing skills.

Warm-Up

Invite children to help fill a shallow pan with water (it will be easier for them to observe if you use a clear or light-colored pan). Ask for a volunteer to squeeze a drop of cooking oil into the pan, using an eyedropper. Ask another child to lay a sheet of paper on the surface of the water and lift it off immediately. Hold the paper up to the light, and discuss what children see. Ask them to hypothesize why the oil remained on the paper.

Activity

1 Explain that children will be using the water pan to create two types of designs using chalk and paint.

2 Put out chalk and strainer. Ask children to use the strainer to gently grate different-colored chalk sticks above the surface of the water. Then invite them, one at a time, to lay their sheets of paper on the surface and lift them off quickly. (Make sure that there is enough chalk dust on the surface each time.) Discuss the results.

3 Refill the pan with fresh water and put out two or three colors of oil-based paint, with a popsicle stick for each color. Ask children, one at a time, to use the sticks to drop paint onto the surface of the water. Suggest that they spread it around for a marbleized effect. Then repeat the paper procedure.

4 Hang children's designs to dry. Then talk about the experiments. Ask children to describe similarities and differences between the two procedures and designs and to compare their results. Display the finished paintings to brighten your room!

Observations

- Do children plan and attempt their own methods of experimentation?

Books

Enjoy books about colors and designs in the world around us.
- *Color Dance* by Ann Jones (Greenwillow)
- *It Looks Like Spilt Milk* by Charles G. Shaw (HarperCollins)
- *Growing Colors* by Bruce McMillan (Lothrop, Lee & Shepard)

SPIN-OFFS

- Pour milk onto plates. Invite children to drop food coloring into the milk and to use straws to blow and mix the food colors. Then add one drop of liquid detergent and watch the colors all run away to the end of the plate!
- Drop different-colored food colorings onto paper towels to create tie-dye pictures. Display their colorful creations for all to see!

Let's Make Bubbles

It's a problem-solving experience.

Materials

- commercial bubble solution and blowing wands
- 2 containers (at least one for each child)
- mop and towels
- pitchers
- spoons and wire whisk
- glycerin
- variety of detergents and soaps, including liquid, dry, and bar

Aim

Children will use problem-solving skills to create bubbles.

In Advance

Set out the materials on a low table in an uncarpeted area. Keep towels and a mop nearby for easy cleanup.

Warm-Up

Invite children to have fun blowing bubbles.

Activity

1 Ask, "What do you think this bubble solution is made of? How can we make our own bubble solution?" Ask children if they remember ever making bubbles when washing their hands or taking a bath.

2 Show children the detergents and soaps and invite them to create their own mixtures. Suggest that they pour water from the pitchers into their dishpans. Invite them to look at and feel the bubble solution you used earlier to help them decide how they want their own mixtures to look and feel.

3 Invite children to try blowing bubbles with their mixtures as they experiment. If they aren't satisfied with the results, encourage them to think about what they can add to make the mixture better. Comparing bubbles made with dry detergent, liquid detergent, and bar soap might help children decide on strategies to try.

4 After children have had time to make discoveries, add the "secret ingredient" — glycerin. Talk about how the mixtures change when glycerin is added.

Remember

- Leave plenty of time for exploration.

Observations

- Note children who think and plan before they try something and those who discover as they go along.

Books

Use these books to further explore bubbles.
- *Bubbles* by Muriel Rukeyser (Harcourt Brace Jovanovich)
- *Bubbles: A Children's Museum Activity Book* by Bernie Zubrowski (Little, Brown)
- *Investigating Science With Young Children* by R. Althouse (Teachers College Press)

SPIN-OFFS

- Put out strainers, collanders, six-pack holders, plastic cups, straws, and paper towel tubes, and invite children to experiment with creating the best blower!
- Keep the detergents and soaps on hand for children to use in dramatic-play activities and to spark discussions about cleanliness and hygiene.

Activity Plans for
Spring

With spring comes a greater interest in the outdoors, weather, air, animals, and plants. The scientific-method skills used in the fall and winter can now be applied at a higher developmental level than at the beginning of the year. Through more defined experiments, children are challenged to investigate complex and abstract science concepts.

Prediction plays a larger role in these activities because kindergartners now have a broader base of experience with science concepts to draw from. Instead of making random predictions based mostly on guesswork, kindergartners are using prior knowledge, observing and comparing new phenomena, and applying this information to their predictions.

Spring activities draw on children's natural interest in growth and change.

Throughout the Day

- Focus on the concepts of same and different and on making comparisons. Help children notice that most things — including themselves — are alike in some ways and different in some ways.
- Talk about nature and the environment. Help children develop an appreciation of and respect for all living things by showing them how the rain, air, animals, and plants are interconnected.

Around the Room

- Display beautiful environmental pictures in several areas of the room to inspire children's dramatic play, block-building, writing, and art.

Color Experiments
Turn your classroom into a color laboratory!

Materials

- different-colored squares of paper
- chart paper and markers
- food coloring
  (limit to red, yellow, and blue)
- 10 clear-plastic cups
- 3 to 6 eyedroppers
- pitcher of water and 3 glasses
- paper towels
- newspaper
- smocks

Aim

Children will observe and experiment with color and absorption.

Warm-Up

Talk about the colors around the room. Ask, "What makes colors? Where do colors come from?" Give children paper squares of different colors and have them find objects in the classroom that are the same color.

Activity

1 Tell children that they can be color scientists. Ask them to fill three glasses with water. Help them add red drops to one glass, blue to another, and yellow to the third to create primary color glasses.

2 Give each child two cups to use for mixing. Let them fill these cups with plain water and then use eyedroppers to get water from the primary color cups. Encourage children to try many combinations. As they mix colors ask, "What colors did you use to make this new color? What is this new color?"

3 Have children predict what will happen if they mix certain colors together. Record children's color predictions on an experience chart.

4 Ask children to test their hypotheses by mixing the colors, and then record their color discoveries on the chart. Are they surprised by their findings?

Remember

- Provide newspaper, smocks, and paper towels so children stay dry.

Observations

- Do children seem to have a plan when they mix colors, or do they mix without careful consideration?

Books

These books will introduce your children to color.
- *Adventures of Three Colors* by Annette Tison and Talus Taylor (C. E. Merrill Pub)
- *Mouse Paint* by Lois Ehret (Harcourt Brace)
- *Little Blue and Little Yellow* by Leo Lionni (Bowmar/Noble Publishers)

SPIN-OFFS

- When children have completed the mixing, give them paper towels to make pictures. Suggest that children place paper towels on newspaper and drip color onto the towels using the eyedroppers. Ask, "What will happen if you drop some of your color on this paper towel? How will it look when it dries?" The dried paper towels are great for doll clothes, play tablecloths, and see-through window decorations.

Let's Make Rain!

April showers will soon come our way!

Materials

- spray bottle filled with water
- dishpans or trays
- soft, thick absorbent sponges

Aim

Children will learn about rain and observe the rain cycle.

Warm-Up

Open a discussion about rain and storms. Talk about the good and bad things rain can do. Make a chart of the comparisons they suggest, Ask, "Where does rain come from? What makes rain?"

Activity

1 Gather children around the water table, or hand out pans to catch their "rain." Give each child a dry sponge. Say, "These are the clouds on a dry day. They are not filled with water vapor." Have children squeeze the sponges. Does anything come out? Why?

2 Lightly spray their sponges with water. "Now your clouds are beginning to fill up with water vapor." Have children squeeze the sponges again and observe the rain come out. Gradually add more and more water to their clouds to produce more rain. As they spray their clouds with water, ask, "what will happen if we add more and more water to the cloud?"

3 Talk about the experience. Explain that even though we can't see it, there's water in the air. It is called water vapor. Sometimes the clouds get so full of this water vapor that they can't hold all of it. When this happens, the water vapor falls to the ground as rain.

4 Encourage children to share their observations of this phenomenon. Have they ever been in a hurricane? Or a snowstorm? Do they think that snow is related to rain? Do they have any theories about what thunder and lightning might be? Encourage speculation.

Remember

- The rain cycle may be difficult for kindergartners to fully understand. It is more important for children to experiment with the process, to offer hypotheses, and to engage in group brainstorming.

Observations

- Do children demonstrate a beginning understanding of the rain cycle? How?

Books

Enjoy these books on rain.
- *Rain* by Peter Spiers (Doubleday & Co.)
- *Where Does the Butterfly Go When It Rains?* by May Garelick (Addison Wesley)
- *James and the Rain* by Karla Kushkin (Harper & Row)

SPIN-OFFS

- Recreate the water cycle. Tape a sealable bag one-quarter filled with water to a sunny window. Watch as water evaporates and condenses at the top of the bag — then falls back again like rain!
- Place different-sized containers on a windowsill. Pour exactly 1 cup of water in each. Ask children to check them over several days to see which container the water evaporates from more quickly. Discuss why this might happen.

Rain Rulers

Celebrate April showers by measuring rainfall.

Materials

- coffee can
- popsicle sticks or ruler
- marker
- chart paper
- construction paper (optional)
- paste and glue

Aim

Children will use science process skills of observation and comparison.

Warm-Up

Talk about the rain, and point out that on some days more rain falls than on others. Ask children whether it is possible to measure the amount of rain that has fallen. Explain that together they will do just that.

Activity

1 Offer children a coffee can to collect rain samples. Place the can in the playground to collect rain. On the day after a rainfall, bring it inside to measure how much rain fell.

2 Stand the popsicle stick or ruler in the can, and ask children to think of different ways they might measure the rain. If they need help, suggest that they mark the top of the wet section of the stick or ruler with a marker.

3 Now ask children how they can record the rain measurement. (One way is to paste the marked stick on the left side of a sheet of chart paper, writing the date below. Or let children cut a bar of the same height out of construction paper and paste it onto the paper.) Encourage children to experiment with a variety of methods.

4 Put the can outside again, and after the next rain, let children repeat the process. Suggest that they compare the two sticks. Ask, "On which day did more rain fall?" Children might repeat the process over a period of weeks to create a rainfall bar graph.

5 Mount the graph in your science center, and use it to force science vocabulary like *precipitation*.

Observations

- Do children enjoy engaging in a long-term project and comparing their findings?
- Do children show creativity in thinking of different ways to measure and record rainfall?

Books

These books will brighten up a rainy day and inspire amateur meteorologists.
- *Hooray, It's Raining* by John Ourth and Mike Sawitz (Good Apple)
- *A Rainy Day* by Sandra Markle (Orchard Books)
- *Rain* by Robert Kalan (William Morrow & Co.)

SPIN-OFFS

- Try keeping a class rain log. Invite children to share things they notice about each rainfall or storm, including the amounts of wind, lightning, and thunder. Suggest that they write and draw their contributions on dated pages.
- Collect pictures of different kinds of weather around the world. Display on walls and label with descriptive titles like "Typhoon," "Hurricane," and "Rain Forest." Encourage children's questions, and help them build vocabulary.

Evaporation Experiments
Where does the puddle go?

Materials

- chalk and/or yarn
- chart paper
- markers

Aim

Children will be scientists as they hypothesize, predict, observe, and evaluate.

Warm-Up

Choose a time after a rainfall to do this activity. Open a discussion about the rain. Ask, "Will the things that got wet in the rain stay wet? What happens to the water?" Ask whether children know the word *evaporation*, and explain that it is the process that dries things when they are wet.

Activity

1 Take children outside and invite them to choose a puddle to observe. Ask, "How fast do you think the puddle will dry up?" Ask them to recall their own experiences with hypothesizing.

2 Give children chalk or yarn and have them mark the outside edge of the puddle.

3 Ask children to predict how much smaller the puddle will be when they come back outside later, and then again the next day. Make a list of each child's predictions on an experience chart.

4 The next day, go back outside to check the predictions. Ask children to hypothesize about where the puddle has gone. Add children's hypotheses to the class chart.

5 Ask children if they think other things might evaporate (such as juice, paint, milk, or even sand). Record their predictions, and then encourage them to test them out in different areas of the room. Do liquids evaporate more quickly on the windowsill?

Remember

- Discourage competition and comparison of whose guess was closest.

Observations

- How do children respond to seeing that the water has disappeared?
- What theories do children have about where the water has gone? Do they connect the sun with the water's evaporation?

Books

These books offer more science fun.
- *Science Experiments & Amusements for Children* by Charles Vivian (Dover Publications)
- *My First Science Book* by Angela Wilkes (Alfred A. Knopf)
- *Dry or Wet?* by Bruce McMillan (Lothrop, Lee & Shepard)

SPIN-OFFS

- Invite children to pour a small amount of water onto a dark sheet of construction paper and watch the paper absorb the water and form a wet area. Then have children trace the outside of the area with chalk. Check the paper the next day, and discuss what happened.

Air, Air, Everywhere
Air is all around us. Can you feel it?

Materials

- bubble-blowing liquid and a bubble pipe
- dandelion that has gone to seed, if possible
- 1 straw for each child
- sheet of paper
- air horn
- beach ball
- hand-held fan
- balloon
- basin of water

Aim

Children will make predictions.

In Advance

Place the following materials on your science table for several days and allow children to experiment with them a blown-up balloon, a basin of water, a straw, bubble-blowing liquid and a bubble pipe, a sheet of paper, an air horn, a dandelion, a beach ball, and a hand-held fan.

Warm-Up

Gather children and talk about how air moves. Encourage them to feel the air moving in and out of their chests as they breathe.

Activity

1 Put a deflated balloon and a beach ball and the other items from your science table into a bag and bring them to circle time. Invite children to take out one item at a time. As they do, help them use air to effect some kind of change. Blow up the balloon and the beach ball, and ask what has gone into them to make them bigger.

2 Invite children to hold their hands over the holes and feel the air rush out. Does it make a sound?

3 Put out other air-related materials for children to experiment with. Ask, "How do you know air is moving? Can you see, taste, or touch it? How?"

4 Record children's findings and their descriptions of air, and then discuss them.

Remember

- Children this age do not need to fully understand all the different scientific concepts and principles that relate to air. It is more important to arouse their curiosity.

Observations

- How do children experiment?

Books

Here are some more science experiments for children.
- *Investigating Science With Young Children* by Rosemary Althouse (Teachers College Press)
- *Mr. Wizard's Supermarket Science* by Don Herbert (Random House)
- *Air* by Robbins (Henry Holt & Co.)

SPIN-OFFS

- Use straws and tempera to male "Airy Pictures." Put globs of paint on paper, and invite children use straws to blow on them. Watch the effect of the air on the painting.
- Make simple kites by folding a large sheet of manila paper in half lengthwise. Open it up, and fold the bottom corners up to the center crease. Staple the flaps together at the corners. Attach a long string and a tail.

Making Wind Indicators
Take advantage of March winds.

Materials

- 2-inch-wide strips of newsprint or colored party streamers approximately 4 feet long
- small objects such as balls, wheel toys, paper scraps, sponges, rocks, foam peanuts, cotton balls
- large sheet of paper
- red and blue crayons
- chart paper
- markers

Aim

Children will participate in a variety of experiments related to the wind.

Warm-Up

Discuss the wind. Ask, "How do you know the wind is blowing? How can we see the direction in which the wind is blowing?"

Activity

1 On a windy day, provide each child with a strip of paper or a streamer. Take children outside and demonstrate how to hold the streamer by one end and let it move in the wind.

2 Have children create their own wind. Encourage them to experiment with waving their arms and running with streamers. Ask, "What happens when you run quickly? Slowly?" Invite children to observe how the streamers look when the wind blows hard and when it is calmer.

3 Go back inside and present a variety of small objects for wind experimentation. Discuss each object. Make a prediction chart and have each child predict whether or not she can move each object by blowing. Make a chart of the children's predictions. Have each child mark off his "yes" predictions with a red crayon and his "no" predictions with a blue crayon. Encourage them to try different positions for blowing or to try "blowing teams." Can they come up with any other suggestions for moving each object?

4 Compare the results with the chart predictions. How many of the predictions were correct? On a windy day, take the objects outside and repeat the experiment. Discuss your results.

Observations

- What do children talk about when discussing the power of wind?

Books

Try these books as a follow-up to the experiments.
- *Play With the Wind* by Howard Smith (McGraw-Hill)
- *The Wind Blew* by Pat Hutchins Viking Penguin)
- *When the Wind Stops* by Charlotte Zolotow (HarperCollins)

SPIN-OFFS

- Make a wind vane by helping children tie a variety of different-weight objects onto a long string, one above the other, with heaviest items at the top. Hang outdoors and watch how the strength of the wind will dictate which objects are blown.
- Learn about windmills — what they are and how they work. You might read books about windmills or even visit one if there's any in your area.

Worm Watching
Let's investigate earthworms!

Materials

- black construction paper
- spoons and shovels
- aquarium
- leaf mulch
- wagon or cart
- cornmeal
- soil
- 10–12 earthworms

Aim

Children will observe worms to learn how they live.

In Advance

After a rain shower, take a walk with children to look for worms. Carefully use spoons, shovels, and hands to scoop up the worms together with surrounding soil, leaves, and other natural material into a bucket. (If you can't find worms, you can buy them at a local bait store.)

Warm-Up

Talk about worms. Where have children seen them?

Activity

1 Put out the supplies and the bucket containing the worms and the natural materials in which you found them. Invite children to touch, feel, smell, and talk about each substance.

2 Together, fill the bottom of the aquarium with about 3 inches of soil. Spread a thin layer of cornmeal on top and about 3 inches of leaf mulch on top of that. Spread another thin layer of cornmeal, and this time top with the worms and the natural materials. Cover it all with a final layer of cornmeal and black paper.

3 A few hours later, invite children to lift the black paper to look for worms. Do they notice any signs that the worms have moved through the layers? Continue to observe the worms over several days.

4 After a couple of days, gently transfer the contents of the aquarium into a wagon or cart and roll it to the area where children originally collected the worms. Together, return the creatures to their natural habitat.

Remember

- Some children might not want to handle worms.

Observations

- Do children treat the worms gently?

Books

Place these books about other earth creatures in your room.
- *The Very Quiet Cricket* by Eric Carle (Philomel Books)
- *One Earth, a Multitude of Creatures* by Peter and Connie Roop (Walker Publishing)
- *The Grouchy Ladybug* by Eric Carle (Crowell)

SPIN-OFFS

- Suggest that children make and keep journals of the worm information they gather. Encourage children to add to their journals as they discover more about worms.
- Create a class story with children contributing ideas about what life would be like if they were worms. How would they feel? What would the world look like? What would they do?

Insect Nets
Let's observe bugs close up!

Materials

- children's insect-reference book
- old pantyhose or stockings, I leg per child
- 3 heavy cardboard discs, about 3 inches across, per child
- natural materials (sticks, rocks, leaves)
- 2-foot lengths of string
- crayons or paint
- scissors
- paper

Aim

Children will make and use insect nets to observe a part of nature.

Warm-Up

On a sunny day, take a walk around your playground or to a park to look for insects. When you notice an insect or spider, try to identify it with the insect guide. Remind children of how important it is to take extra care not to disturb the insect or its surroundings.

Activity

1 Help children cut off the legs of the pantyhose. Hold the toe down and help children stuff a cardboard disc inside to create a floor for their net. Stuff another disc about halfway down, and use the third disc for the roof of the net. Tie the excess hose in a knot over the third disc, and cut a slit — just big enough for a child's hand to fit through — above the floor of the net.

2 Each day invite one or two children to hang their nets from low tree limbs and jungle gym bars using the lengths of string. When children find an interesting creature, help them carefully place it and some of its surroundings through the slit in the side of their net.

3 Invite everyone to watch the insects during the day. Notice close up how they move and eat. Look for different body parts. At the end of the day, be sure to take your visitors back where you originally found them.

4 After children free their insect, suggest that they draw or paint the insect. Place a few sticks, rocks, leaves or other natural items in the nets with the drawings and hang them in your science center for an interesting bug zoo.

Observations

- Note children's feelings about bugs. Are they afraid to touch them or even look at them?

Books

These bug books will get your scientists thinking!
- *The Big Bug Book* by Margery Facklam (Little, Brown & Co.)
- *Pet Bugs: A Kid's Guide to Catching and Keeping Touchable Insects* by Sally Kneidel (John Wiley)
- *A Creepy Crawly Song Book* by Hiawyn Oram (Farrar, Straws and Giroux)

SPIN-OFFS

- Put a variety of food crumbs on a plate and place on playground. Watch to see which foods ants are attracted to. Children can even predict beforehand.
- Provide pipe cleaners, wire, foam packing peanuts, tissue paper, and other small items children can use to create their own pet insects. Ask each child to write a short story about their bug.

Magnifying Nature

A tiny seedling is a sign that nature grows.

Materials

- large freestanding magnifier (this usually comes on a wooden tripod for preschoolers)
- several small shatterproof magnifying glasses
- experience-chart paper
- markers
- paper
- clipboards

Aim

Children will use observation and recording skills as they look for signs of nature's young.

Warm-Up

Share the book *Everything Grows* by Ruth Krauss. Look closely at the pictures and notice how plants, trees, animals, and people grow and change. Afterward, make a list together of things that grow.

Activity

1 On a sunny day, gather your magnifying glasses and a few interested children for an outside adventure. Ask, "Do you think we can find tiny things that grow?" Explain that everyone will need to look carefully because some of nature's babies are very small and delicate. They can look for tiny plants, eggs, flowers, or baby animals. Remind children that the magnifying glasses will make the small things look bigger.

2 Take time to explore. Get down on all fours to check in the grass, under rocks, and in flowers beds. Look for flower buds just popping out, new shoots of grass between the longer blades, birds' nests, buds on tree branches, and tiny white eggs on ant hills. As you find nature's babies, be careful to observe but not disturb them.

3 Provide paper and markers for children to record their observations.

4 Come back over time to look at and record changes in the young.

Remember

- Help fives realize that they are bigger than some things, that they are much bigger now than when they were babies, and that being small can be important.

Observations

- Note children's different techniques in drawing what they observe.

Books

Place these books about spring and growing on your science table.
- *Animal Babies* by Harry McNaught (Random House)
- *Animal Babies One Two Three* by Eve Spencer (Raintree Steck-Vaughn)
- *In Just-Spring* by e.e. cummings (Little Brown)

SPIN-OFFS

- Invite a parent with a young baby to visit regularly, and observe the baby's growth monthly. Record with drawings and writing in an "Our Class Baby" journal!
- Collect a variety of nature and parenting magazines, and suggest children identify and cut out pictures of plant, animal, and people babies. They can use them to create a "Nature's Young" collage!

What Do Birds Eat?

Help your group find out!

Materials

- 2 sheets of experience-chart paper
- marker
- string
- crayons
- blunt needles

Aim

Children will develop environmental awareness.

Warm-Up

Take a walk and observe birds and their behavior. Back in your room, encourage children to share what they have learned about birds. Record their responses on an experience chart.

Activity

1 Label a second chart "What We Think Birds Eat," and invite children to make suggestions. Record the foods children suggest next to their names, and encourage them to draw a picture of the food next to the words.

2 Over the next few days, ask children and parents to help you collect the suggested foods for an experiment. Once you have them, offer each child a piece of string with a large blunt needle threaded through one end. Encourage children to string a few pieces of each food.

3 Help them hang the chains from low tree branches, where birds can reach them easily but small animals can't. If possible, choose a tree just outside a window so children can watch the birds eat.

4 Hang your chart at children's eye level near the window. Throughout the day, encourage children to observe which foods the birds ate (or are eating now!) and which are still there. Demonstrate how to check off foods on the chart as they are eaten. After a few days of observing, gather your group again to talk about which foods the birds chose.

Remember

- Some foods can be dangerous for birds to eat, such as peanut butter, which can spoil in warm weather, and rice. Keep a list of these as you learn about birds, and remind children not to use them in their experiment, and why.

Observations

- Note children who have a strong affinity for nature.

Books

Here are some great bird reference books for children.
- *Birds* by J. Grabianski (Franklin Watts)
- *Elizabeth the Bird Watcher* by Felice Holman (Macmillan)
- *Birds Eat & Eat & Eat* by Roma Gans (HarperCollins Children's Books)

SPIN-OFFS

- Examine old nests to see materials used by birds to build nests. Then invite children to choose materials to put outside on branches or a fence. Watch to see what the birds use.
- Encourage children to notice what their pets (and their own family members) eat over the course of a week. This might offer a good opportunity to discuss healthy eating habits.

The Power of Plants

It's amazing how strong seedlings are!

Materials

- small clear-plastic cups
- potting soil
- large, fast-growing seeds, such as lima beans or squash
- variety of items such as paper, cardboard, cloth, burlap, pebbles, small rocks, and dry plaster of paris.

Aim

Children will use observe, predict, experiment, and problem-solve.

In Advance

Prepare a chart to record predictions and results. On the left side of the paper, make a list of the different materials you will test. Draw a simple picture cue next to each one.

Warm-Up

Take a walk to observe evidence of plant growth in unusual places. Look at the edges of pavement and on sidewalks, driveways, gravel walks, even stone patios. Observe the ways the seedlings grow.

Activity

1 Back in your setting, ask, "I wonder if we could get our seeds to push up through any other materials?" Show children the different materials you have collected, and ask them to suggest other items they would like to test.

2 Help children plant a few seeds in each cup, water them, and place one of the experimentation materials on top of the soil. If you're using plaster of paris, help children mix a small amount into a paste and pour it over the top of the planted and watered soil. Then ask children to place the cups in a sunny window.

3 Ask children to predict whether their seedlings will be able to push up or through the materials. Invite them to mark their initials under the column that represents their predictions. Check plant pots each day.

4 After the plants have grown, go back to the chart and record the results of the planting experiments. Compare the predictions with the results.

Remember

- Be sure to water the seeds well before covering them.

Observations

- What information do children use to hypothesize?

Books

Here are some books about growth.
- *A Seed Is a Promise* by Claire Merrill (Scholastic Inc.)
- *How a Seed Grows* by Helene Jordan (Thomas Y. Crowell)
- *Up Above end Down Below* by Irma Weber (HarperCollins)

SPIN-OFFS

- Explore how the sun helps plants grow. Place grown plants by a window and watch how they grow toward the light. Turn them around and watch them grow toward the light again.
- Put some seedlings inside a closed shoe box with a hole at one end. Water regularly, but keep the lid on. Observe what happens over time.

Let's Be Gardeners
Plants grow from seeds.

Materials

- large plastic margarine tubs, old plastic dishpans, berry baskets
- packets of seeds for plants such as herbs, miniature vegetables, and small annual flowers
- sphagnum moss (from garden shop)
- large spoons or small shovels
- screwdriver
- potting soil
- markers
- container of water
- roll of masking tape
- experience-chart paper

Aim

Children will experience planting seeds and the responsibility of caring for their plants.

In Advance

Ask parents to donate margarine tubs, old dishpans, and berry baskets.

Warm-Up

Gather children and talk about gardens. Ask, "What kinds of things grow in a garden?" Invite children who have a garden at home to talk about what they grow in it, and how. What steps come first, next, and last?

Activity

1 Bring out all the materials. Ask children, "How can we use these items to create a garden?" Invite each child to choose a container or basket to use as a planter. Help children use a screwdriver to carefully punch holes in the bottom of the plastic rubs and dishpans.

2 Ask children to help you place the moss in a container of water. Let it soak until thoroughly wet. Drain the water and invite children to use the moss to line the inside of their planters. Explain that the moss will help the plant grow because it will allow more air and water into the soil.

3 Ask children to use the shovels to fill their planters with soil. Help each child plant seeds according to the package directions. Use masking tape and markers to label each plant. Then place the plants in a sunny spot.

4 Make a list of garden responsibilities for each child on an experience chart, and encourage everyone to pitch in. Make another experience chart to list the weekly changes children see in the plants.

Observations

- How do children approach the process of planting?

Books

Read these books along with your gardening activity.
- *Backyard Sunflower* by Elizabeth King (Dutton Children's Books)
- *A Flower Grows* by Ken Robbins (Dial Books)
- *Kids Garden!* by Paul Mantell and Avery Hart (Williamson)

SPIN-OFFS

- On a sheet of paper, list the type of seed that each child planted. Then help children make a graph to show the growth rate of each plant. Talk about which plants are growing quickly and slowly.
- Have children draw and write about their own plants, and compile their drawings to make an "Our Garden" class book.

Planting Terrariums

Create a "piece of the earth."

Materials

- large clear-plastic cups or plastic shoe boxes
- potting soil
- gravel or small stones
- shells
- bark
- plastic wrap
- spray bottles
- small houseplants or cuttings, moss, and ferns
- small toy animals and people (optional)

Aim

Children will use observation, experimentation, and prediction skills as they create a natural setting.

In Advance

Collect cuttings from your own plants at home. Invite families to send in cuttings too. A local florist might also donate small cuttings.

Warm-Up

Open a discussion about pollution and garbage and the importance of taking care of the earth. Ask children if they can think of examples of pollution. What is pollution? How does it affect plants, fish, animals, and people? Why do people litter? Then explain that together you will make terrariums, which are like little Earths.

Activity

1 Talk about what the earth is made of and what you see when you dig in the ground or when you walk in a garden. Show children the plant cuttings.

2 Help children carefully place a small amount of gravel in the bottom of their plastic containers and then slowly add soil, stones, shells, and bark.

3 Have children carefully place one or two cuttings in the soil, and remind them to be sure that all the roots are covered with soil. Ask children to lightly spray the plants with water. Place your terrariums in a sunny window and watch them grow.

4 Help children observe that plants need water and sunlight. Ask them to predict what would happen if you put one of the terrariums in a closet. Invite children to test their predictions.

Observations

- Note children's fine-motor skills as they work with small items in small containers.

Books

Here are some books about plants and protecting the earth.
- *The Little Park* by Dale Fife (Albert Whitman)
- *The Tree* by Donald Carrick (Macmillan)
- *Wilson's World* by Edith T. Hurd (HarperCollins)

SPIN-OFFS

- Use a plastic shoe box or a glass aquarium to make a bigger class terrarium. In this larger space, children can create hills and valleys and add props to create a scene. Keep in the moisture by covering the top with plastic wrap, and spray only when the dirt appears dry. Add visiting insects, if possible.

Activity Plans for
Summer

Their store of scientific knowledge has brought children to a new level of awareness about the outdoor environment. This often leads to an interest in observing and protecting nature. In these summer activities, children take science back outside for a look at the effects of the sun and a study of the environment.

Their learning comes full circle back to the autumn's investigations of self and the world…but now children are at a higher level of understanding. As they explore their bodies, this, time in relationship to their world, they will use all the science and thinking skills they have acquired throughout the year and will be amazed at how much they have grown and learned.

In the summer, the sun can play a central role in children's science investigations.

Throughout the Day

- Help children notice not only how they've grown but how other parts of the school environment have changed. Go back to the tree you observed in the fall to note changes.
- Talk about positive change and negative change. Help children become aware of the effects of pollution on plants, animals, and on themselves.

Around the Room

- Collect different artists' interpretations of the sun, and display them around the room for inspiration and discussion.
- Put out a variety of nonstandard measuring devices for children to use to measure natural and human-made objects.

Pollution Scientists

Let's "look at" litter!

Materials

- paper bags or lunch bags (one per child)
- crayons or markers
- collage materials
- glue
- scissors
- chart paper
- disposable vinyl or plastic gloves

Aim

Children will become aware of the effects of litter and pollution on our environment.

Warm-Up

Talk about litter. What is it? What does it do to the environment? Where do you find litter? What is it made of? Look outside the window for examples of litter, or bring in some examples from outside to examine. Ask, "What are some of the things we can do to stop litter and pollution? How can we help in our own neighborhood and classroom?" Explain that together you will design your own bags for collecting litter.

Activity

1 Provide a bag for each child. Encourage them to use crayons or markers and collage materials to decorate them. Write children's names on the bags.

2 Explain that you will take the bags on a litter hunt. Discuss the types of litter that are acceptable to touch. Then ask, "Where will we find the most litter?" Record the types of litter children think they will find.

3 Take a walk around the playground and school neighborhood. Collect "clean" litter. Look for the predicted items as well as for types of litter that were not suggested. Point out noticeable effects of the litter on the area. Ask, "What are some things we can do to prevent pollution?"

4 Go back to the classroom, and compare the contents of the litter bags with the prediction chart. Sort and classify the trash into categories such as wood, paper, plastic, etc. Glue some of the trash onto paper and set up an anti-litter bulletin board.

Remember

- Remind children to wear gloves when collecting garbage and to wash hands when they are through.

Observations

- Do children show sensitivity to pollution?

Books

These books will inspire more talk about the environment.
- *About Garbage and Stuff* by Ann Z. Shanks (Viking)
- *The Cleanup Surprise* by Christine Loomis (Scholastic Inc.)
- *What Happens to the Garbage?* by Rona Beame (Messner)

SPIN-OFFS

- Use art materials and recycled materials to create anti-litter posters to place around the school neighborhood.
- Help children set up a recycling center far your classroom. Mark large cartons with labels such as "Paper," "Plastic," "Glass," and so an. Before throwing trash away, ask children whether it might be recycled. At the end of the year, take a class trip to your local recycling center.

What's in the Air?

We can make "air detectives" to find out.

Materials

- chart paper and marker
- wax paper
- petroleum jelly
- tape or stickers
- hole puncher
- string or yarn
- hand-held magnifiers

Aim

Your children will use observation, experimentation, and evaluation skills.

Warm-Up

Bring children outdoors and begin a discussion about what is in the air. Suggest that they take time to notice things in the air. When you come back indoors, record their ideas on experience-chart paper. Explain that you will create air detectives to learn more about what's in the air.

Activity

1 Invite children to spread a thin layer of petroleum jelly on pieces of wax paper to make air detectives. Ask for suggestions of places to hang them to test the air. Encourage them to think of a variety of places, such as next to the school building, near a driveway or parking lot, and hanging from a tree.

2 Bring the air detectives outdoors, along with tape, a hole puncher, and string or yarn. Let children place or hang the air detectives in the spots they suggested, and label them with their locations.

3 The next day, collect the air detectives. Bring them back to your room and use a magnifier to look at the contents closely.

4 Ask children to write or draw descriptions of what they see. Together, try to identify some of the particles by looking in books and studying the flowers, shrubs, and trees outside. Return the detectives to their locations and check them again after one week. Which locations have the most plant materials? Which have the most dirt? Encourage children to hypothesize about the reasons for the results they found.

Observations

- What knowledge about air pollution do children exhibit?

Books

These books teach respect for the earth.
- *Caring for Our Earth* by Carole Greene (Endow Publishers, Inc.)
- *Caring for Our People* by Carol Greene (Enslow Publishers, Inc.)
- *Eco Art! Earth-Friendly Experiences* by Laurie Carlson (Williamson)

SPIN-OFFS

- Investigate water pollution by collecting water samples from schoolyard puddles. Pour the water through coffee filters. Observe and record residue and colors.
- Have children brainstorm all the things that might pollute our air or water and ways they can imagine or invent to clean it up.

Me and My Shadow

Step into the sun for a shadow-measuring activity!

Materials

- colored chalk
- mural paper
- yarn, string, plastic links, tape measure, and other measuring tools
- scissors
- masking tape
- markers or crayons

Aim

Children will use the skills of measurement, estimation, and prediction to experiment with their shadows.

Warm-Up

On a sunny day, go outside together or let lots of light into your classroom. Then go on a shadow hunt. Look for shadows made by trees, play structures, furniture, and, of course, people. Then ask children to pair up to trace and measure their shadows.

Activity

1 Show children how one child in each pair can stand in the sun on a hard surface (or on mural paper if you're inside), while the other child uses chalk or a pencil to trace the shadow.

2 When children finish, ask them to trade places so everyone has a shadow tracing. Suggest that they write their names in their shadows.

3 Encourage children to think of ways to measure the shadow, then invite them to test their ideas. Have a variety of measuring tools handy, such as yarn, string, and plastic links.

4 Help each pair measure their shadows using the material or tool they chose. One child can hold the yarn or other material at the head of the shadow tracing while the other stretches it to the bottom. Then help them cut it so that each child will have a length of material that represents the length of his or her shadow.

5 Encourage children to predict whether their shadow lengths are longer than, shorter than, or the same length as their own bodies, others' shadows, and other objects they see. Show them how to measure lengths of materials against the objects to test their predictions.

Observations

- How much did children in each pair cooperate and share ideas during the activity?

Books

These are some shadow books you can share:
- *The Biggest Shadow in the Zoo* by Jack Kent (Parent's Magazine Press)
- *Buddy's Shadow* by Shirley Becker (Jason & Nordic)
- *Clare and Her Shadow* by Jeffrey Severn (Chronicle Books)

SPIN-OFFS

- Play shadow tag! Instead of tagging each other's body, children can tag each other's shadow. Who's "it"?
- Suggest that children create a story or movement activity about being a shadow. If they were a shadow, what would it be like? What would they want to say and do?

Make a Shadow Clock

Shadows can tell time.

Materials

- chalk
- coffee can
- dirt or sand
- 2-foot stick or dowel
- 8 stones
- tempera paint

Aim

Children will investigate shadows and how they move.

Warm-Up

Invite children to look for shadows around the room. Encourage children to experiment so they begin to understand that shadows are formed when the light is blocked.

Activity

1 Hang a simple shape in a sunny window so that its shadow makes a clear silhouette on the floor. First thing in the morning, gather together and use chalk to outline the shape's shadow. An hour later, check to see where the shadow is. Mark its new position throughout the day.

2 Explain to children that long ago people told time by the movement of the shadows made by the sun over the course of a day. Explain that they are going to build their own shadow clock.

3 Ask children to fill the coffee can with moist sand or dirt and then press a stick firmly into the center of the can. Move the can to a sunny area of the playground or by a sunny window. Place a small stone at the top of the shadow made by the stick. If it's about 9:00 A.M., help children paint a 9 on the stone.

4 One hour later, check to see where the shadow of the stick appears and mark it with a new stone. Add the new numeral to represent the new time. Repeat this process every hour to create a shadow clock for the hours of your school day. The next day, check to see if the clock is still accurate. Share the findings.

Remember

- Give children experiences with the movement of shadows and opportunities to observe the changes.

Observations

- Do children connect the shadows with the sun?

Books

Read these books about shadows.
- *Come Out Shadows, Wherever You Are* by Bernice Myers (Scholastic Inc.)
- *The Owl Who Was Afraid of the Dark* by Jill Tomlinson (Viking)
- *Play With the Sun* by Howard E. Smith (McGraw-Hill)

SPIN-OFFS

- Invite pairs of children to trace each other's shadow at different times of day in the same place on the school pavement with large, colorful chalk. Do the shadows change size and shape?
- Invite children to share experiences with other kinds of timekeeping devices they've seen (such as stopwatches, kitchen timers, watches, hourglasses, etc.). Provide a variety of these tools and encourage children to explore them freely.

Shinin' Through

Choose a sunny day for this prediction activity.

Materials

- variety of objects such as light- and dark-colored construction paper, cardboard, rocks, leaves, and books
- chart paper
- red and green crayon

Aim

Children will develop an awareness of the sun and of the concept of transparency.

In Advance

Prepare a sunlight prediction chart by dividing a large sheet of chart paper into five vertical columns. Divide the columns horizontally to form as many boxes as you have objects in your experiment. Use the other columns to mark predictions (yes/no) and results (yes/no).

Warm-Up

On a bright, sunny day gather children together outside. Encourage everyone to talk about the sun. How does it feel? What does it do?

Activity

1 Ask children whether they think the sun can shine through objects. Encourage them to search for objects that light shines through. Notice windows, leaves, and screens.

2 Back in the room, hold up each of the items you collected and ask children whether they think the sunlight will shine through them. Help them record their predictions on the chart. Offer a green crayon to check the "Yes" column and a red crayon to mark the "No" column.

3 Test the predictions by holding each object up to direct sunlight. (Remind children to focus on the object and not to look directly at the sun.) Mark the result in the appropriate column. When all of the objects have been tested, compare the predictions to the results. Ask, "Why do you think the sunlight shines through some items and not others?"

4 Invite children to use their new-found knowledge to search for an item they think will let sunlight through and an item they think will not. Allow plenty of time to test out these new predictions.

Observations

- What information do children base their predictions on? How do they test their hypotheses?

Books

Use these books to "light up" your class!
- *The Sun's Day* by Mordicai Gerstein (HarperCollins)
- *Arrow to the Sun* by Gerald McDermott (Pullam)
- *Sunny Days & Starry Nights* by Nancy Fusco Castaldo (Williamson)

SPIN-OFFS

- Make sunlight pictures by placing dark construction paper on a sunny windowsill. Invite children to collect interesting flat objects to arrange on the paper. Leave them in the sun for a week. Then remove the objects and look at the shadow pictures you created. Encourage children to hypothesize about what happened to the exposed construction paper when it was left in the sun.

Sun-Powered Cooking
Let's use the sun's heat to make snacks!

Materials

- large bowl
- aluminum foil
- plastic knives or spreaders
- paper plates and napkins
- peanut butter (refrigerated)
- cheese   ■ crackers

Aim

Children will investigate solar power.

Warm-Up

On a sunny day, talk about the warmth you feel from the sun. Ask, "What can you tell me about the sun? What does it do for us? How do people use it? Has anyone ever cooked with the sun? How is an oven like the sun?"

Activity

1 Continue the discussion, explaining that the sun's power can even melt foods. Explain that you will use the sun to melt peanut butter to spread on crackers.

2 Make a solar oven by lining the inside of a large bowl with aluminum foil. Place a glob of cold peanut butter on the bottom of the bowl, and position the bowl in direct sunlight so that the sun's rays are shining on the inside of the bowl. You may need to use blocks to prop the bowl at an angle to catch the rays.

3 Let the bowl sit for about an hour and encourage children to make periodic checks of the melting progress. Then help children spread their melted peanut butter on crackers and serve for a simple picnic treat.

4 Put a slice of cheese on one cracker and some stiff peanut butter on another. Ask children to predict which they think will melt first. Then find other items to melt, such as an ice cube, crayon, and birthday candle. Record on a chart the time it takes each item to melt, and compare children's predictions.

Remember

- Be sure to talk about safety when using the sun's power. Point out the danger of some metal objects getting too hot to touch. Remind children that foods such as cheese can spoil in the sun.

Observations

- Do some children feel uncomfortable about eating something that's been cooked in a different way?

Books

Here's some good sunny-day reading.
- *The Day the Sun Danced* by Edith T. Hurd (HarperCollins)
- *Everything Changes* by Ruth R. Howell (Atheneum)
- *Sun* by Michael Ricketts (Grosset & Dunlap)

SPIN-OFFS

- Make sun tea by placing two herbal tea bags in a clear, quart-size glass jar. Fill the jar with water and cover it tightly. Give children time to observe what the tea looks like. Place it in the sun for two to three hours. Encourage children to observe the changes in the water as well as the changes in the way it smells. Record the color changes on a chart. Then serve the tea chilled with lemon along with some tasty crackers for your hungry solar scientists!

Wake Up, Earth!
Let's be "dirt scientists"!

Materials

- small shovels or trowels
- large plastic or glass jars (or an aquarium)
- chart paper
- watering can
- plastic wrap
- magnifying glasses
- drawing paper
- crayons
- markers

Aim

Children will observe, compare, and record changes in soil and develop environmental awareness.

Warm-Up

Talk about changes that happen outside during April. Most areas will see new growth occurring and changes in the soil, even if there is no actual springtime. In some places, the earth seems to sleep during winter and come alive in spring.

Activity

1 While on the playground, have children help you use trowels to dig a clump of ground (at least a 6-inch cube) to study. Dig deep enough to get a few layers of soil. Place the clump right-side up inside a container (an old aquarium works best).

2 Inside, have children observe the soil. Ask them to describe what they see. What color is the soil? Are there any worms? Insects? Pebbles? Write their ideas on an experience chart and date it.

3 Water the soil, cover it with plastic wrap, and place it near a sunny window. Periodically, have children use magnifying glasses to observe the changes that occur in the soil. Record their observations on dated charts. As the earth warms, new plants, bugs, and worms will appear.

4 Have children keep an observation log with drawings and dates of observed changes as they appear.

Remember

- Talk about the importance of washing one's hands whenever working with soil.

Observations

- Are children developing an appreciation of caring for plants, animals, and the earth? How is this manifested?

Books

These books raise environmental awareness.
- *The Mountain* by Peter Parnall (Doubleday)
- *Blue and Beautiful Planet Earth, Our Home* by Ruth Rocha and Otavio Roth (United Nations Publishers)
- *Kids' Nature Book* by Susan Milord (Williamson)

SPIN-OFFS

- Suggest that children become dirt detectives. Their job is to investigate different soil samples and compare them. Give children plates, plastic spoons, sieves, magnifiers, and soil samples. Ask them to examine the soil, talk about the things they find in it, and then make a list of them. Look for signs of pollution and non-natural items. Then make sure children wash their hands.

Be a Rock Hound

We'll have "mountains" of fun!

Materials

- variety of rocks and pebbles
- magnifying glasses
- markers
- chart paper
- white paper and pencils
- paper bags
- paper plates
- egg cartons
- pan balance

Aim

Children will observe, compare, and classify rocks.

In Advance

Ask parents to donate egg cartons and paper bags and to help their children gather rocks and pebbles that can be contributed to a class rock collection. To gather more rocks, go on a collecting walk with children. Give each child a paper bag, and encourage everyone to look for rocks and pebbles of different sizes, shapes, and colors.

Warm-Up

Gather children in a circle outside, and look over the rock collection together. Explain that they can work in small groups to study and experiment with the rocks.

Activity

1 Help children divide into groups, and give each group a mound of rocks and pebbles. Encourage children to use magnifying glasses to make close observations.

Ask, "How are the rocks the same or different? How many shapes, sizes, and colors do they come in?" Give each group a chance to share what they found.

2 Invite children to sort the rocks in any way they choose — by size, texture, shape, color — onto paper plates. Once they are finished sorting, ask them to describe the rocks on each plate.

3 Make an experience chart describing the different ways children classified the rocks. Then invite them to count the rocks on each plate. Together, discuss which plate has the most and which has the fewest rocks.

4 Ask children to arrange the pebbles from smallest to largest in an egg carton. Give out sheets of white paper and pencils, and let children trace the smallest and largest pebbles and compare the differences.

Observations

- What different criteria do children use to sort and classify the rocks? Can they find more than two ways to sort and compare them?

Books

These books will enhance your rock study.
- *Rock Collecting* by Roma Gans (HarperCollins)
- *On My Beach There Aye Many Pebbles* by Leo Lionni (Astor-Honor)
- *Everybody Needs a Rock* by Byrd Baylor (Macmillan)

SPIN-OFFS

- Let children use a pan balance to compare the weights of various rocks. Ask them to predict which rocks will be the heaviest and which the lightest. Then ask them to test their predictions.
- After studying and experimenting with the rocks, create a rock museum. Display the rocks in your science center, and provide signs that describe the biggest, smallest, roughest, smoothest, etc. Invite parents to visit the rock museum.

As Big as Me

What things are just my size?

Materials

- yarn
- scissors

Aim

Children will use their bodies as a unit of measure.

Warm-Up

Open a discussion about the different ways children have grown this year. If you took measurements at the beginning of the year, compare them with children's measurements now. Encourage children to bring in clothes or shoes that are now too small for them and compare them with the clothes they are wearing now.

Activity

1 On a sunny day, take the children outdoors and open a discussion about growth. Ask, "What else grows like you?" Look for signs of growth in plants and trees in your area. Explain that new growth appears as the light areas of bright green on the ends of branches and plants.

2 Ask children to look for the plant that has the most new growth on it. Suggest that they use lengths of yarn to measure how much the plants have grown.

3 Invite children to separate into pairs. Encourage one child to lie down on a clean area, while his or her partner measures his length using a long piece of yarn.

When one partner has measured out the length, help him cut the yarn. Then ask children to trade places.

4 Next, invite pairs to search the playground together as "measuring teams," measuring the size of other objects using their pieces of yarn. Can they find something on the playground that is bigger than they are? Smaller? The same size? Then ask partners to show the group the different-sized objects they found.

5 Suggest that children draw pictures or write in their journal about the things they found that were the same size as them.

Remember

- Be sensitive to children who may not have grown as much as their classmates. Discourage children from making comparisons of size.

Observations

- How has children's understanding of measurement changed since the beginning of the year? Are they more careful or accurate?

Books

Share these storybooks about growing.
- *Big Enough* by Myra Anderson (DOT Garnet)
- *The King's Flower* by Mitsumasa Anno (Putnam)
- *George Shrinks* by William Joyce (HarperCollins)

SPIN-OFFS

- Suggest that children bring in old clothes and shoes that no longer fit them to show each other how they've grown.
- Help children tie all their yarn pieces end to end and find a thing to measure that's as long as the whole class!